Dear Romance Reader,

Welcome to a world of breathtaking passion and never-ending romance.

Welcome to *Precious Gem Romances*.

It is our pleasure to present *Precious Gem Romances*, a wonderful new line of romance books by some of America's best-loved authors. Let these thrilling historical and contemporary romances sweep you away to far-off times and places in stories that will dazzle your senses and melt your heart.

Sparkling with joy, laughter, and love, each *Precious Gem Romance* glows with all the passion and excitement you expect from the very best in romance. Offered at a great affordable price, these books are an irresistible value—and an essential addition to your romance collection. Tender love stories you will want to read again and again, *Precious Gem Romances* are books you will treasure forever.

Look for fabulous new *Precious Gem Romances* each month—available only at Wal★Mart.

Kate Duffy
Editorial Director

A GIFT OF LOVE

Deborah Matthews

Zebra Books
Kensington Publishing Corp.
http://www.zebrabooks.com

To Nancy Jenkins for her friendship and encouragement.

And to Beverly Beaver, who introduced me to Romance Writers of America and the ladies of the Heart of Dixie Chapter.

ZEBRA BOOKS are published by

Kensington Publishing Corp.
850 Third Avenue
New York, NY 10022

Copyright © 1999 by Deborah B. Matthews

All rights reserved. No part of this book may be reproduced in any form or by any means without the prior written consent of the Publisher, excepting brief quotes used in reviews.

If you purchased this book without a cover you should be aware that this book is stolen property. It was reported as "unsold and destroyed" to the Publisher and neither the Author nor the Publisher has received any payment for this "stripped book."

Zebra and the Z logo Reg. U.S. Pat. & TM Off.

First Printing: November, 1999
10 9 8 7 6 5 4 3 2 1

Printed in the United States of America

One

An angel he was not. Unless he had been cast out of heaven. Too handsome by far, he looked like one of the devil's own.

Dorie tugged her black-and-white pony to a halt. A body lay half-in, half-out of a brook crusted with ice.

Jumping from the rough cart, Dorie ignored the wooden sliver that pierced her glove as she dashed to the lifeless form—a giant of a man in a multi-caped greatcoat and black Hessian boots, stretched out in the frozen snow.

Black lashes shadowed cheeks that were as pale as the snow that dusted him. He had the look of a man who enjoyed life. He was not dissipated or stout, but an aura of frequent, frivolous gaiety seemed to cling to him.

Dorie pushed her sliding spectacles back onto her nose and stooped to study him. A knot of purple, swollen flesh marred the stranger's temple. Tugging one glove off, she clasped his bare hand, white and waxy from exposure to the wintry weather. Bone-deep cold met her fingers.

A pain-filled groan escaped him, making Dorie's heart race.

He was alive!

The giant shivered violently. She leaned over him and shouted, "Can you hear me?"

Eyelids fluttered open, revealing onyx eyes that did not focus. "Egadth, the dead can hear you. Where am I?" he mumbled, and his eyes closed again.

Dorie replaced her glove, rubbed her hands together to warm them, and replied, "Apparently, you've had an accident. We need to get you out of the snow."

He ignored her undeniable observation.

Dorie tugged on his arm, but the giant did not budge. "Stand up and I'll help you to my pony cart. Where do you live?"

His brow furrowed and confusion threaded his voice. "Live? I-I'm not thertain."

What in the devil was she to do with this large stranger? Leaving him to the mercy of the elements was out of the question.

Dorie sighed heavily. "I guess I'll have to take you home with me."

A warm smile played on his lips and he looked at her through half-open lids. "Thounds 'lightful."

Her eyes narrowed suspiciously at his slurred speech. "Are you foxed?"

"Don' think tho. Can't theem to 'member." His voice trailed off into a thin whisper.

Clutching him under the armpits, Dorrie huffed, "Try to stand up."

Slowly, the man managed to come to his feet, but swayed forward. Dorie clutched his shoulders. The biggest man she had ever seen, well over six feet, towered over her. "Easy. Can you walk?"

His head bobbed up and down like a toy in the wind. "Ever sinthe I was a young lad." His hands began fumbling with his greatcoat fastenings.

"What are you doing?" Dorie demanded.

"Taking off my clotheth."

Grabbing his hands with hers, Dorie said, "Not now. You must walk to the cart."

"You're a regular little shrew ordering me about. Like a bloody general. Are you related to Wellington?"

Dorie groaned. "I think you're addled." Positioning herself under his arm, she said, "Lean on me and walk."

Heeding her directive, he sagged against her. Heavily. Dorie thought she would collapse under the unwieldy burden. He must have weighed sixteen or seventeen stone.

But he smelled nice, like pine and horses. The fragrance surrounded her like a cloak.

Dorie swallowed with difficulty; her heart thundered in her ears.

They finally arrived at the cart after what seemed like an eternity. He thudded on the wooden floor and Dorie winced. At least he was now inside. Unfortunately, there was nothing in the cart for a warm cover.

She regarded him with sober curiosity. Ceaseless questions churned in her mind. Who was he and what brought him to Yorkshire? Had an accident befallen him, or had someone deliberately harmed him?

Dorie pushed her ponderings aside and climbed

aboard the cart. Clucking to the pony, she said, "We're ready, Matilda." The pony walked slowly across the half-frozen stream and turned left.

A dismal Christmas awaited the Knighton family this year. Dorie sighed wistfully as a cold more bitter than the Yorkshire weather spread through her soul once again. The harsh realities of life and loneliness were her companions since her father's death two years ago, but her sister maintained stars in her eyes and hope in her heart, certain that Christmas would be joyful and magical.

Dorie did not mind so much for herself, but disappointment would find Hannah next week. At nine, Hannah had not yet learned that magic and angels did not exist in the real world.

Crisp air singed her cheeks and she inhaled deeply of the clean scent. The snow had stopped for the moment. The sun shone palely through the veil of grayish clouds, as if through frosted glass. Shimmering ice crystals clung to bleak branches now stripped of their leaves. This December was turning out to be colder than usual.

New-fallen snow painted the countryside a winter wonderland, an angel's playground. At least according to Hannah. But all Dorie felt was bitter cold and a wish to return to the warmth of her cottage. No matter how bright the fire, though, the warmth did not spread to her heart or her soul.

Snow began to swirl around the pony cart, making a blinding white screen as the wheels crunched and churned on the country lane. Icy fingers of winter stroked her cheeks and needles of frosty air pricked and stung. How much snow must they endure?

Dorie shivered against the frigid weather. She

pulled the knitted scarf further up her face and clucked to her pony, urging her to go faster. The day was not fit for man or beast, and now she must attend this injured stranger.

Dorie pulled the pony cart to a halt in front of her cottage. The door flung open and Hannah bounced out. "Where have you been so long, Dorie? We were getting worried."

Dorie smiled at her sister. Curly hair surrounded her face and her coat had been slung on haphazardly. "I'll explain later." Dorie jumped from the cart and pointed to the back. "Help me get him inside."

Hannah peeked over the side of the cart and her eyes grew large. "Who is he?"

"Please, no questions now. I don't know how long he has lain in the freezing weather."

Hannah and Dorie tugged on his arms and managed to get him to his feet. His eyelids fluttered open and he looked from one side to the other.

Hannah smiled at him. "What's your name?"

"Angelth," he murmured.

Hannah stared wide-eyed at him.

"Hush," Dorie instructed as they stumbled to the door.

The door opened and rounded eyes peeped out. "You're bringing him inside?" an anxious voice whispered.

Dorie looked into her aunt's gaunt, wan face and felt a twinge of guilt. Rose's bosom quivered with nervousness and her gray hair stood on end as if she had seen a ghost. Aunt Rose would be scandalized at what must be done.

That is if she remembered longer than a second. Aunt Rose had become occasionally forgetful in her old age and sometimes wandered off, unable to find her way home.

Some advised Dorie to send Rose away to Bedlam, but she refused. Horror stories abounded of the insane asylum.

Dorie inhaled deeply and fortified herself to be firm. "I have no other choice, Aunt Rose. He's half-frozen."

Closing the door behind them, Rose informed her, "H-he's a man."

"I know. He will not harm you." Dorie's spectacles fogged up and her feet stumbled over a rug. "Aunt Rose, take my spectacles off before I do us bodily harm."

Rose did so and followed behind the threesome.

They managed to get him to the first bedchamber and eased him onto the bed. "Hannah, run to fetch Doctor Acker."

Dorie took her spectacles and rubbed the glass lenses with the edge of her gown.

Rose shook her head. "I saw Mrs. Acker in the village this morning. The doctor departed early to deliver Mrs. Radford's baby. She doesn't expect her husband until tomorrow or the next day."

Dorie sighed, replaced her spectacles, and looked at Hannah. "Then leave a message with his wife that we have someone who needs immediate attention."

Hannah nodded and dashed out of the room.

Rose hovered nearby, wringing her hands. "What do you plan to do?" she asked in a nervous whisper.

Dorie stiffened, momentarily abashed, but courage and determination welled in her. "Take his clothes off and warm him."

The shocked gasp reverberated around the room. "Dorie, you mustn't. 'Tis not proper."

Dorie whirled to face her aunt. "Would you have me let him die? Propriety can go to the devil."

"N-no, but someone else . . ."

Dorie stripped off her gloves, scarf, coat, and bonnet, laying them on a side table. "Who? You?"

Rose's face blanched white. Dorie smiled kindly at her aunt and patted her hand.

Turning Dorie's hand over, Rose gently touched the red swollen skin where the wooden sliver had lodged. "We must remove the splinter."

"After I've attended the stranger. Please warm some bricks, Aunt Rose, and find one of Papa's nightshirts. I can handle things here."

Rose nodded and raced from the room as if the hounds of hell nipped at her heels. Dorie chuckled and turned back to her patient. Dangerous eyes glittered as he studied her from beneath hooded lashes. The heat scorched her down to her toes. "I do not believe a lady hath ever thripped me before without my permission." A shiver wracked his body and his teeth chattered.

Heat flooded Dorie's cheeks and she attempted to ease her embarrassment. "I'm trying to help you, sir. You're wet and half-frozen."

A smile covered his face, displaying straight white teeth. He reminded her of a wolf ready to devour her. He held out his arms. "Thtrip away, my lady. My only requetht ith you warm me with your body. Body heat ith betht."

"We shall remove your boots first," Dorie said, ignoring his comment. Boots that had long ago lost their shine. They were wet and covered with mud. She grabbed hold of one boot and pulled. It did not budge a fraction.

"You need better leverage," the man instructed. "You'll find it eathier from the other way 'round."

Dorie's forehead knitted and she asked, "Other way around?"

He nodded his head and then winced. "With my boot between your legth."

Dorie's face burned hotter. He was right. All the times she had removed her father's boots, that was the way she'd accomplished it. But she was loath to present her backside to this man's view. If only he would stay unaware of his surroundings.

Swallowing hard, Dorie swung her foot over the stranger's leg and quickly removed the boot. Thankfully, there was nothing forthcoming from her patient.

She quickly straddled his other leg and yanked on the boot. As the boot was halfway off, a low, husky voice said, "Nithe view."

Dorie lost her balance and thudded to the floor. She sputtered, "Really, sir!"

He only grinned and shrugged. "You'd have me tell a lie?"

"No, I would have you keep quiet," she huffed.

"Beg your pardon, my lady." He chuckled and closed his eyes again.

Trembling hands fumbled with the buttons on his greatcoat. Dorie chewed her bottom lip and admonished herself. *There is no reason to be nervous. I'm doing my duty toward this gentleman. It is the only alternative since the doctor is not available.*

And his clothes definitely labeled him a gentleman. Dorie dropped his greatcoat to the floor. Though crumpled and soiled, his stylish clothes were of the finest quality. She tugged off his once-snow-white cravat, blue coat with gold buttons, and striped waistcoat, dropping them on top of the greatcoat.

The door creaked open. Only Rose's head came through the door, leaving the rest of her body outside. "What was I supposed to get?" she asked, her eyes limp and liquid.

Dorie patiently reminded her. "A nightshirt, and place some bricks in the fire."

Rose nodded. "I-I'm sorry, Dorie. I won't forget again."

"It's no problem, Aunt." The door creaked closed.

Once again alone, she inhaled deeply and contemplated the man. An inherent strength lined his face, with an aquiline nose and generous mouth. His hair was a mass of elflocks, matted and tangled in a riot of confusion. A single swath of hair fell casually on his forehead.

She almost had him undressed and was not sure what to do with an unclothed man. Especially one in her own bedchamber. Heat infused her face at the thought of a man here in her sanctuary.

The fire popped and Dorie jumped, afraid for a moment she had been caught staring at him.

The door opened slowly and Dorie turned. Two fingers holding a man's nightshirt eased through the door. Rose said, "Here's one of your father's nightshirts."

Dorie walked to the door and grasped the shirt. "Thank you, Aunt Rose."

"I have the bricks in the fireplace."

"Thank you."

The door clicked with only a whisper of sound. Dorie smiled. Time to get on with her task. There was no reason to be embarrassed.

She turned back to her patient. Dark eyes scrutinized her. Suspicion hovered on his brow. "What do you plan to do with that awful nightshirt?"

"Put it on you."

He scowled. "I don't wear nightshirtth."

"You can't remember your name nor where you live, but you know you don't wear nightshirts? You must wear something."

"I assure you one doeth not have to wear anything thleeping." His scowl deepened. "Thtrange indeed that I remember that, yet do not know my name or what happened to me." His eyes cut back to the nightshirt. "Will your huthband not mind?"

Dorie ignored the heat burning her cheeks once again. It seemed to be a common occurrence today. "I have no husband. This was Papa's. D-do you think you can manage the nightshirt yourself?"

"Thertainly don't want to offend your maidenly thenthibilitieth," he muttered, and sat up on the edge of the bed. His torso swayed.

Dorie stepped forward and put her hand on his shoulder to steady him. Heat burned through the fine lawn and scorched her hand. Of its own accord, her hand jerked away and she met his gaze. A satisfied smirk lingered in his unfathomable eyes. She finally managed to wrench her gaze away.

At seven-and-twenty, she rested firmly on the shelf. She had always found herself quite content there. But nothing in those twenty-seven years prepared her for the intimate proximity of this man and the strange emotions he awoke.

She gulped as the stranger's hands fumbled with his shirt. "Bloody hell," he cursed, "I'm ath uncoordinated ath a babe."

Grabbing hold of his shirt, Dorie jerked it off and dropped it on the stack of clothes. Her breath caught in her throat at the unfamiliar sight. A large expanse of bronzed skin and wide shoulders filled her gaze. Black hair was sprinkled over his chest, disappearing into the waist of his breeches.

Dorie briskly tossed the nightshirt over him. His head appeared through the neckhole and he gazed at her, his tousled hair making him look like a little boy. She balled her fists to fight the urge to straighten his hair, all the time wondering if the ebony locks would feel like cool silk.

He pushed his arms through the sleeves and the nightshirt tail pooled around his hips. Falling back onto the bed exhausted and pale, he mumbled, "Can't do any more." His eyes languidly closed.

Thick, coal black lashes cast deep shadows across his cheekbones. The thin nightshirt tightened and strained across his chest as if the cloth would rip apart at any moment.

With one finger, Dorie poked his shoulder. "Sir?"
Nothing.
"Please, sir, can you not discard your breeches?"

Now, that was one request she had never expected to make.

His only response was a deep gulp of air and a snort.

Dorie examined her options. She could leave his breeches on, but they were wet. Or she could be brave and relieve him of the snug, almost indecent, piece of clothing.

Dorie's face burned at the thought of undressing the man further. Even if it was only for his health.

Not that she would really *see* anything. The nightshirt covered his private parts. Parts unknown to her. She hurriedly pushed that thought away. Now was *not* the time to appease her curiosity.

Lifting the nightshirt hem, Dorie squinched her eyes tight and worked the first button free. A quiver of movement brushed her fingers. She gasped and drew back. What in the devil?

She hesitated. Using only two fingers, she grasped the edge of the nightshirt and raised it inch by inch. But she saw nothing.

Thankfully the stranger kept his eyes firmly closed, unaware of what was taking place and unable to make any comments.

Releasing the nightshirt to allow it to pool around his hips once again, she gathered her courage. Shutting her eyes, she continued. Her fingers groped for the next button, found it, and loosed it.

Once again a movement fluttered against her fingers. Gasping, Dorie jerked away and stared. Had some animal burrowed into the man's breeches while he lay unconscious in the snow?

She chewed on her lower lip and wondered what

A GIFT OF LOVE

to do. For the first time in many years, she was at a loss as to what action to take.

Gently with one finger, she poked the unusual creature. She drew back and watched in anxious curiosity as it swelled and grew larger, doubling in size. Was there more than one creature?

Dorie glanced around, searching for something with which to cudgel the interloper when she freed him from his prison. She grabbed up the shovel from the fire irons. Returning to the bed, she drew it back, ready to whack the animal.

The stranger's eyes opened slowly, then widened in horror, snapping black fire. She sensed the barely controlled power coiled in his body. His hands instinctively covered himself and his curt voice lashed at her. "What in bloody hell are you doing?"

Two

A long, brittle silence followed. Dorie lowered the fire iron, her mind whirling in bewilderment. "I . . . there . . ." She inhaled deeply and tried to marshal her thoughts. It was almost impossible under the intensity he radiated toward her. "You passed out and I was attempting to undress you so I can put you to bed."

His brows flickered. "I'm flattered you felt compelled to strip me and get me into bed."

Blood pounded in her temples. "It's not like that, sir," she huffed. "Your condition requires warmth and dryness."

"And the fire iron?"

"There . . . there seemed to be something alive in . . . in . . ."

"Alive?"

"Something moved against my finger."

He stared at her for a moment, his mouth an O of surprise. Throwing back his head, he roared with laughter, deep and full-hearted. "You were about to diminish my ability to produce children," he sputtered between his laughter.

"Are you laughing at me?" she demanded in irritation, both hands on her hips.

His laughter sobering, he said, "Not at all, Miss . . . ?"

"I'm Pandora Knighton. Everyone calls me Dorie."

"As in Greek mythology?"

She nodded. "Papa was the local schoolmaster and a great student of the ancient Greeks."

"As I recall, Pandora could not contain her curiosity and unleashed disaster on the world."

"Yes," she whispered.

"Where am I?"

"In Yorkshire in my cottage. I-I didn't know where else to take you. Dr. Acker is away from the village."

"I believe we're acquainted well enough for me to call you Dorie. If you will give me a few minutes alone, I shall finish undressing myself."

Dorie nodded and flew from the room, suddenly anxious to escape his amusement. Every fiber in her being whispered alarm, but she was glad to be unaware of the full explanation of what had occurred. She suspected this was one of those matters of which they strived to keep young women ignorant. But just what did it have to do with children?

He lay back in the bed. The bricks had warmed him nicely, but his mind was still a blank. He possessed no idea of who he was or how he came to be in Yorkshire with a wound on his head. Had his horse thrown him? Did he even own a horse? No answers were forthcoming. But at least he no longer slurred his words.

Surveying the small chamber, he wondered of Dorie's circumstances. Threadbare draperies hung at the window and no carpet covered the rough wooden floor. Very little existed in the way of furniture. The bed he reclined in, a table with a candle and pitcher, and a very small wardrobe were the only items.

Miss Dorie Knighton was something of an enigma. She took a strange man into her home knowing nothing about him except that he needed assistance. And from the looks of things, she could ill afford another mouth to feed.

No doubt about it, Dorie was a plain, drab little wren. Hair tied back in a severe chignon. Spectacles camouflaging eyes as blue and clear as the sky. Gown faded and worn. What would she look like dressed fashionably with her hair less severe? Would she blossom into a brightly plumed bird?

Utterly ridiculous, he told himself, *to think such thoughts. It is none of my concern.*

A soft knock sounded at the door. "Enter," he called.

Dorie walked in and smiled. "How are you feeling?"

"Nice and cozy."

"I brought you a cup of warm broth."

"Broth," he said in disgust. "How about a nice glass of brandy or port?"

"I'm sorry, but I don't have spirits in the house."

He sighed, propped himself on the pillows, and accepted the chipped cup. "Thank you."

"Have you remembered anything?"

Frowning, he shook his head and sipped the chicken broth.

"Aunt Rose was cleaning your clothes and found this in a pocket." Dorie held out a piece of vellum.

A GIFT OF LOVE

He took the paper and examined it. There was evidence there had once been a red wax seal, but it had broken off. He read the note:

> *Ash,*
> *Glad you're coming to visit us during Christmas. See you on Monday.*

The vellum had been torn where a name might have been signed.

"Do you recognize the name?"

Disappointment twinged inside him. Would he ever remember anything? "No, but I must be Ash. An odd name, though."

"Not really. At least we have something to call you, Ash. Er, Mr. Ash."

"Ash will do nicely. We are rather intimate friends after all."

Her face flushed with embarrassment and her gaze searched for somewhere to rest. Apparently, she was uncomfortable looking at him.

"Was there anything else in my pockets?"

"No."

"No money?"

Dorie shook her head.

Of course, if his pockets had contained anything valuable, it was possible she had decided to keep it. He admonished himself for such thoughts. This woman had saved his life. He could at least believe her.

A whisper interrupted their conversation. "Dorie."

An older woman hesitated in the doorway, a handkerchief twisted between her hands. "Dorie, Doctor Acker is here."

"Thank you, Aunt Rose. Come in, Doctor."

A tall, slim man entered the room, his face drawn. Wispy gray hair adorned his head and he clasped a black bag in his hand.

"How is Mrs. Radford?" Dorie asked.

"She and the babe are both fine. Delivered a healthy girl." The doctor turned his gaze to Ash. "Sorry I couldn't come before now, but Mrs. Radford had a hard time of it."

Ash nodded. "Miss Knighton has been taking good care of me."

Doctor Acker turned to Dorie and asked in clipped speech, "What did you do?"

"I saw that his wet clothes were removed. Then, put him to bed with plenty of covers and hot bricks. I've been feeding him warm broth and tea. Oh, and I cleaned his head wound and salved it with ointment."

Doctor Acker nodded. "Sounds as if you did everything right, my dear. I'll examine him now, if you don't mind leaving us alone."

"Of course. If you need anything, let me know." She shut the door quietly behind her.

Doctor Acker placed his bag on the table and began his examination. "How long did you lie in the snow?"

"I don't know," Ash answered.

"What were your symptoms in the beginning?"

"I slurred my words and, according to Miss Knighton, my skin was waxy and cold."

Doctor Acker massaged Ash's hand, and then probed the purple flesh on his forehead.

"The slurred speech would be from the knock on

A GIFT OF LOVE

the head. No organs seem to have been permanently damaged."

"About my memory?"

The doctor settled onto the foot of the bed. "We don't know much about memory loss. I've seen it last a couple of days and I've seen it last years."

Ash held out the note. "Someone was expecting me for Christmas."

Doctor Acker studied the note and nodded. "I'll ask around and see if anyone knows of you." He rose and patted Ash on the shoulder. "Don't despair, my boy. We'll find out who you are. Would not be at all surprised if your memory returns in a few days."

Laying the note on the table, the doctor picked up his medical bag. "There's no reason you can't be up and about now."

"What is your fee? I don't wish to be a burden to Miss Knighton."

Doctor Acker rubbed his chin as if in deep thought. "Do you have money?"

"Miss Knighton discovered none in my pockets. Otherwise, I don't know."

The doctor smiled and patted the scarf around his neck. "Miss Dorie has already paid me, sir, with this fine woolen scarf and a tea cozy for Mrs. Acker."

"Scarf and tea cozy?" he asked in bewilderment.

"Miss Dorie is a fine hand at knitting. I know it's not the way of city folks, but we country people take care of each other best we can. Not that Miss Dorie accepts anything smacking of charity. But I allow her to pay my bills with her knitting."

Ash nodded. "That is kind of you, sir."

"Her father was an old friend. Sorry to see her

and Hannah in such dire circumstances, but as I said, Miss Dorie accepts nothing akin to charity. If you have need of me, don't hesitate to send Hannah."

Ash stared after the doctor as he departed. But he had no time to consider anything. A young voice piped up from the door. "May I come in?"

He smiled at the child. "Of course. Perhaps you would like to read to me after you have introduced yourself."

Hannah made herself comfortable on the foot of bed and said, "Later. I'm Hannah, Dorie's sister. I must talk to you."

Settling back into the warm comfort of the bed, he asked, "What do you wish to talk about?"

She wrapped her arms around her knees and said quite matter-of-factly, "You being an angel."

Three

Hannah's face and blue eyes glowed with wonderment. Under her steady scrutiny, Ash found himself at a loss for words. He might not know who he was, but something innate told him he was no angel.

A grin overtook his features and he replied, "I'm not an angel, Hannah. What makes you say such a thing?"

Hannah's smile disappeared. "When Dorie brought you home, I asked your name. You said angel."

"What was happening at the time?"

"Dorie and I were on either side of you helping you inside."

"I'm sure I meant the two of you were angels."

Hannah reached into her pocket and drew out a piece of vellum that had been folded and refolded many times. "You *must* be the angel come because of my letter."

He held out his hand and asked, "May I?"

Hannah nodded and gave him the paper.

Dear Christmas Angel,

Dorie takes good care of me and Aunt Rose, but she has no love in her life. She worries so much about making sure we have everything we need and works much too hard. I haven't heard her laugh once since Papa's death. It would mean ever so much to me if you would bring her some love and happiness. A good start would be new knitting needles, a new coat, ingredients for the wassail bowl, and a new gown for the earl's party. Best of all would be a kind, loving husband.

And let Dorie change her mind about attending the Christmas party at the earl's estate. She never has any fun.

I would be ever so grateful if you can make Dorie happy once again.

And if you see my Mama, tell her I said hello.

*Love,
Hannah*

Ash's throat tightened with emotion. The letter was so unselfish. Ash was not sure how he knew, but some instinct told him this sort of unselfishness was unusual. He refolded the vellum and tried to collect his emotions. In a gruff voice he asked, "Who is the Christmas angel?"

Joy filled Hannah's face. "I was born on Christmas Day. Mama said that made me special, with my very own Christmas angel. So, I thought if I wrote a letter, the angel would answer it and make Dorie happy."

"Surely there is something *you* would like to have."

Hannah shrugged. "Nothing important."

"Come now. What would *you* ask for if you could have anything you desired?"

"A new coat." Hannah's thumb creased her patched gown that might have once been a rich brown, but was now a pale imitation. "And new skates."

"Do you enjoy skating?"

Her face, framed with curly brown hair, glowed with pleasure. "Oh, very much. Dorie and I used to go skating on the earl's pond every year."

"And you don't any more?"

The pleasure died from her face, replaced by implacable determination. "I outgrew my skates and we can't afford new ones, but life will be different one day when my angel calls."

Ash leaned forward and asked softly, "And if you never see this angel?"

Hannah smiled at him as if he were a small child who had just questioned the existence of God. "But I will. Though I may not actually see him."

"Him?"

Hannah nodded. "In the Bible all the angels are men. Gabriel. Michael."

"Hannah, you should not disturb Ash," Dorie chided from the doorway.

"She's not disturbing me. The doctor said I could be up and about. If I had my clothes . . ."

Pointing across the room, Dorie said, "They are in the wardrobe."

"If you ladies will excuse me, I believe it is time I walked around."

Dorie said, "We were about to sit down to luncheon, if you would like to join us."

Ash smiled. "Sounds wonderful. I shall join you shortly."

Hannah grinned and clapped her hands together.

"I'm so glad you're feeling well enough to get up." She jumped up and rushed out.

Dorie followed Hannah and softly closed the door.

Ash wished he really was a Christmas angel with the capability of assisting this small family. But somehow he knew he did not believe in fairy tales and he certainly was no angel. He was not quite certain how he knew, but nonetheless discerned it to be an undeniable fact.

The aroma of fresh-baked bread wafted on the air as Ash walked into the cottage's main room. His mouth watered at the thought of a good meal. Three pairs of female eyes turned to look at him.

He grinned and held out his hands. "Thank you for cleaning my clothes and boots."

"Aunt Rose is the one responsible. Ash, my aunt, Mrs. Rosalind Dorrington."

A thin, sixtyish woman attired all in black stared at her hands in her lap as if the last thing she wanted was to meet him. Gray hair was almost hidden by a lace cap.

Ash crossed the room and bowed over her. "My thanks, Mrs. Dorrington."

Rose blushed and giggled. "You're most welcome, sir. I'm only sorry I could not get a nice shine to your boots."

Dorie gestured to the table. "Shall we eat?"

Ash rubbed his hands together. "Something smells appetizing."

It was a simple meal of mutton, potatoes, bread, and apples. When Ash had popped the last bite of bread into his mouth, he leaned back.

A GIFT OF LOVE

"Thank you for the delicious meal."

"You're welcome. How are you feeling?" Dorie asked.

"Much better. Perhaps I should go to an inn."

"But you have no money," Dorie reminded him. "You're welcome to stay here a few days. Your memory may return in that time."

The idea made him feel guilty for being a burden to this family. But what else could he do? Nothing came to mind. "Very well, but I would like to repay your kindness in some way."

"That is not necessary, Ash."

"Dorie, I must insist."

"But how?"

"I'm capable of work." Ash looked at his hands. They were smooth and uncallused. The hands of an idle man. But he had to find a way to repay their kindness. They could ill afford their generosity. "I can at least carry coal, clean the grates, and stoke the fires."

Dorie smiled. "Do you know how to black a grate?"

Did he? He searched his memory and found no inkling of how to go about the task. His hand tightened on his knee. "No, but I'm sure if someone explains it to me once, I can comprehend. And for the meals, I can slice potatoes and apples. I have no wish to be a burden."

"That's very commendable, sir," Rose murmured. "So many young men are rakehells of the lowest order."

Suddenly, a huge ball of white fur bounded onto the table. Startled, Ash jerked back. Narrow blue eyes inspected him as if the weight of the world rested on the cat's conclusion.

"Down, Snowflake," Dorie ordered, but the feline ignored her and continued to stare at Ash.

Hannah snatched the animal from the table. "Bad kitty," she gently scolded. Hugging the cat to her, Hannah stroked his head and met Ash's gaze. "You'll have to pardon Snowflake. His manners aren't very good," she explained.

He nodded, amazed once again at the strange household in which he had come to reside. Ash searched his memory for some snag of information on his identity, but nothing was forthcoming. It was as if some unseen hand had wiped the slate of his mind clean, leaving no trace.

Gently, he probed the swollen lump on his forehead. Had he hit his head upon a tree limb or had he fallen from his horse? Or was it something more sinister?

He shook his head and silently chastised himself. There was no reason anyone would want to harm him. Was there?

The flickering firelight cast shadows across the room, driving off the frigid cold of the winter evening. Outside, the wind howled and snow blustered.

A ball of white fur coiled in front of the fire, gently purring. Snowflake lay on his favorite pillow and savored the warmth.

The shadows hid some of the shabbiness, but Dorie knew each tiny section of the room by heart. The aged fabric of the settee and chairs was thin and shiny, the wooden arms nicked and dented. A hairline crack stretched across the mantle.

Dorie sighed silently and shifted position in the wingback chair. She cut her eyes toward her companion and wondered what he thought of the cottage.

Eyes closed, Ash leaned his head on the chair back. His midnight black hair gleamed almost blue. His face was pale and lean, and purple still adorned his forehead. His presence loomed large and intimidating in the cottage.

After Aunt Rose and Hannah had retired for the evening, Dorie settled by the fire to knit. Remarking that he was not ready for sleep, Ash had joined her. Yet he looked as if he now slept snug and peaceful, ensconced in the chair next to her.

Conversation had been sporadic. Still, there was a peacefulness between them, rather than an awkward silence.

"Are you going to stare at me all night?" His deep voice tumbled over her.

Dorie's face flushed and burned with embarrassment. Gads, what must he think, with her staring at him like a starry-eyed young girl?

"I thought you ill," she fibbed, unable to admit she had been staring, or that her thoughts had been far from sympathy.

Eyelids fluttered open and his black gaze scrutinized her. "I'm fine. My head no longer pains me."

Dorie forced a smile. "That's good."

For a moment, Ash watched as her hands moved the needles back and forth, back and forth, knitting the blue yarn, the click-click-click steady and sure.

"What are you making?"

"A scarf. Mr. Cranley at the village shop purchases my knitting."

"I'll go into the village tomorrow."

Dorie's hands stilled. "Do you think you should? Perhaps you should rest another day."

Ash shook his head. "I feel fine. I must go. Something or someone may spur my memory." His hands tightened on the chair arms. "You can't understand how it feels to know nothing about yourself."

"I'm sure it is dreadful to have your memory erased. Doctor Acker said you could recall everything at any time. I know more of it than you know," she whispered.

"You have lost your memory at one time?"

"No." She debated whether to reveal the truth to him. "Aunt Rose can be forgetful at times. Doctor Acker says it is her age and nothing can be done about it."

"It is commendable that you take care of her."

"There have been some who thought I should lock her up in Bedlam, but it seems cruel. She has very lucid moments." Dorie shivered. "I have heard so many horror stories of the place."

"Why did you take me in?"

"I could not leave you to die."

"But I'm a stranger. I could murder you in your bed."

Dorie shrugged. Before she could answer, the door shuddered under a pounding knock. She dropped her knitting into her lap and stared at the door. Who would be knocking on her door in the middle of the night during a snowstorm?

Four

"Would you like me to see who it is?" Ash asked.

Dorie shook her head and nudged her spectacles up.

Snowflake meowed and stretched his back into a curve. He perched on the pillow and studied the door with narrowed eyes. Strangers were always unwelcome to Snowflake.

Dorie stood and laid her knitting in the chair. Pulling her shawl closer around her, she stepped to the door and readied herself.

A wintry blast of frigid air blew into the room. Candles flickered and danced in the maelstrom, trying desperately to extinguish themselves. The covered doorway kept the snow from entering.

Dorie shivered and motioned the bundle in. He almost looked like a highwayman with a scarf wrapped around his face and a hat pulled low over his eyes. She closed the door and turned. Tense and alert as Snowflake, Ash kept his black gaze on the stranger like a cat ready to pounce and defend.

Slowly, the figure unwrapped. First, his gloves and hat revealing a tousle of red hair. Then, the scarf that covered the lower portion of his face exposed a bushy red beard. His greatcoat remained in place.

He smiled and said in a brogue, "I be sorry to disturb ye. I've had a wee bit of an accident. May I stand by the fire and be warming myself? The night is verra cold."

"Of course," Dorie answered and reclaimed her chair.

Striding to the fire, the stranger clasped his hands behind his back and faced them. "Allow me to introduce myself. I be Angus McLaren. Again, I apologize for disturbing you and your husband, Mrs . . ."

On his stomach, Snowflake crept to the offending boots in front of his fire and sniffed. He snarled and hissed.

Startled, Angus looked down.

"It's Miss Knighton. And you will have to forgive Snowflake. He doesn't like strangers."

Angus's gaze shifted between Dorie and Ash and understanding dawned in his eyes. A wicked grin covered his face and his eyebrows danced.

"Wipe that smirk off your face or I'll do it with my fist," Ash threatened, his voice dark and dangerous.

Angus's face became blank and he bowed. "I meant nae offense, sir. I was going back home to Scotland and have met with a wee accident. I was thinking I could make it home before the storm set in, but my horse is near frozen. Seeing your lighted window in the darkness, I made my way here. I wasna sure how far the next town might be and dinna want to freeze to death. My wife will throttle me if I dinna make it home to her."

Dorie contemplated the man. Not quite as tall as

Ash, he seemed . . . nice enough. She could not very well throw him back into the storm to freeze to death. And Ash was present. He would keep her safe.

Dorie smiled. "You're welcome to stay here . . ."

Ash interrupted her. "Dorie, may I speak with you a moment?"

She looked to Ash and forced her smile up a notch. "No, you may not." Turning her gaze back to Angus, she said, "You're welcome to sleep here before the fire. I have no extra bedchamber."

"Aye, I can make do anywhere, Miss Knighton. I am accustomed to roughing it. We Scots are made of strong stuff. Yer hospitality is appreciated a muckle amount."

Dorie hugged her knitting to her breast and stood. "I shall fix you a pot of tea and a bite to eat. Then I shall leave you gentlemen for the evening."

Angus grabbed one of her hands and Dorie jumped in surprise. Ash came to his feet, coiled and ready to strike. Angus squeezed her hand and said, "Ye're an angel, miss."

"There is a small stable behind the house. Feel free to stable your horse there." Dorie paused at the door and looked back where Ash still stood ready to pounce. "Behave yourself, Ash, and make my guest welcome," she admonished.

The words Ash muttered under his breath were indiscernible, but Dorie suspected it was a blessing they remained so. All of a sudden, Ash seemed dark and dangerous, not at all the lighthearted fellow she had carted home two days ago.

* * *

Angus smiled, revealing even white teeth, his eyes still on the door Dorie had disappeared through. "Verra nice lady."

Ash continued to scowl. "Too much so."

"Ye dinna need to worry, sir. I ken ye wish to protect the lady's reputation. I'll no be telling anyone of yer presence in the lady's house. Or my own." Angus removed his greatcoat, threw it over the back of the chair, and settled down.

"It's not exactly a secret since the doctor has called on me, but I do wish to protect Miss Knighton."

"Aye, that be a nasty bruise on yer noggin. How were ye wounded?"

Ash stared into the fire and gently probed his bruise. "I'm not certain. I remember nothing before Miss Knighton found me in the snow and brought me here."

Angus tsk-tsked. "A sorry shame. Ye must be wretched remembering nothing."

Nodding, Ash asked, "Do you intend to stable your horse?"

"I took the liberty before I knocked. My horse dinna like the weather a wee bit."

"You're a bold fellow to take so much for granted."

"Aye, I be a Scotsman." Angus tilted his head and scrutinized Ash. "Ye look familiar to me."

The beating of Ash's heart froze at the statement and his hand clutched the chair arms. "You think you know me?" he whispered.

Angus stroked his beard. "I canna place ye, but I vow I've seen yer features afore."

"Do you travel regularly to England?"

A GIFT OF LOVE

"Aye. To Yorkshire, Herefordshire, and Dorset quite frequently. My wife is from Dorset."

"You married an Englishwoman?"

"Aye. She's a bonny lady, but keeps me on me toes. Every man should be married. There's nothing more joyful. Our first bairn be due in February."

"Congratulations," Ash said, but his voice showed his lack of conviction.

"Ye doubt me?"

"Yes, but I'm not sure why. I have no knowledge of my own marital state."

But somehow he did not *feel* married. Surely he would sense a wife and children.

A staccato drumming filtered through Ash's consciousness. He glanced down at his fingers tapping on the chair arm. He balled his fingers into a fist, forcing himself to abort the mindless gesture.

"Many a buck dinna feel the need unless they want something. An heir or a fortune. But marriage be a grand state."

Ash said, "I believe I'll retire. Do you need anything?"

"Nay, I have my plaid and that's all I need."

Ash nodded and strolled to his bedchamber. Angus was certainly a proponent of marriage, but he knew little else about the stranger. It was just possible Angus would murder them. Ash decided he best stay awake the night.

Morning sunshine, warm and bright, filtered through the curtain. Last night's storm had dissipated during the night, leaving the countryside shrouded in white.

A rustling sounded behind Dorie and she turned from the window, a piece of vellum clutched in her hand. Hannah stretched her arms above her head and peered at Dorie from the edge of the counterpane.

"Mornin', Dorie. I heard a strange man's voice last night."

"Good morning, Hannah. A traveler seeking shelter from the storm came to the door."

Hannah's eyes opened wide. "Did it snow again?" She sprang from the bed, ignoring the cold floor under her bare feet, and dashed to the window. "It did snow again! It's so beautiful."

Dorie smiled indulgently at her little sister. "I suppose so."

Hannah's gaze fell on the vellum. "What do you have there?"

"The invitation from Lord and Lady Thorley. I-I was just reading it again."

"Have you decided we may go?" Hannah asked, hope evident in her voice.

Dorie shook her head. "I'm sorry, Hannah, but as I explained earlier, we can't go. We have nothing appropriate to wear."

"But we have gowns," Hannah argued.

"Faded and threadbare gowns." Dorie smoothed the skirt of her faded blue gown and turned back to the window. "Nothing fine enough to wear to such a grand soirée."

"But Dorie . . ."

Dorie turned from the window and held up her hand. "Not another word, Hannah. We have already

A GIFT OF LOVE

discussed this. Now, get dressed and help me with breakfast."

Dorie quickly exited, not wishing to discuss the topic any longer. Hannah simply did not understand that people of genteel poverty like themselves did not rub elbows with peers of the realm.

Dorie was also disappointed. It seemed like eons since she had attended a party or laughed. Once she thought her destiny would take a different path, but one took what was given and survived. All that mattered was that Hannah was well and healthy. After all, there were no angels or knights to rescue her from her fate.

Much to her surprise, Dorie entered a toasty warm kitchen. The fire blazed brightly. It was she who usually kindled the kitchen fire, but not today. Obviously, someone had beat her to the task. And the guilty one was busily positioning the copper kettle on the stove.

Ash looked up from his chore and smiled. "Good morning. I heard you and Hannah talking, so I figured you would be out shortly."

Dorie's face burned with embarrassment. Did he know *everything* she did? She pushed the thought away and asked, "Where is Mr. McLaren?"

"He departed at first light. The snow had stopped and he was anxious to get home. He asked me to thank you again for your hospitality and he left something." Ash pointed to a small bag lying on the table.

The heavy bag jingled and clanked as Dorie picked it up and drew the drawstring open. Pouring the contents into her hand, she stared at the silver coins.

Ten shillings. A small fortune.

"Why did you allow him to leave this?" she whispered.

Ash shrugged. "I did not know what the bag contained. Most would be thrilled and thankful for Angus's generosity."

Dorie glared at Ash. "I do not accept charity."

"I'm sure Angus did not leave it for charity. Merely his way of thanking you for giving him sanctuary from the storm. Do you plan to ride to Scotland to give it back?" Ash asked with a raised eyebrow.

A startled inhalation came from the doorway. Dorie's gaze swung to find Hannah and Aunt Rose.

Hannah rushed forward. "Oh, Dorie!" One hand tentatively touched the coins. "How wondrous. We can purchase new gowns to attend the earl's party."

Dorie's hand closed around the coins and she quickly threw them in the bag. "Nonsense. I cannot ride to Scotland as Ash suggests to return the money, but we will spend cautiously," Dorie declared.

"But, Dorie . . ."

"Hush, Hannah. No arguments," Dorie softly ordered.

Guilt immediately consumed her. Hannah looked so disappointed.

Rose said, "Surely, a small luxury will not hurt."

"We will treat ourselves to something. Perhaps a Twelfth Night cake or a plump Christmas turkey." Dorie's fingers brushed Hannah's cheek. "How does that sound?"

Hannah's voice sounded small. "Whatever you

think best, Dorie," she said, and raced out of the room. Rose followed behind her.

Dorie stared after her and murmured, "She doesn't understand."

A large hand settled on her shoulder and Dorie jumped at the unexpected touch. His warm breath ruffled her hair. "She's still young. One day she will thank you for everything," Ash comforted.

The heat of his touch burned through the wool of her gown. Her toes instinctively curled and she labored to breathe. His nearness was like a blanket smothering and baking her wits.

She finally managed to mutter, "I hope so."

His hand gently squeezed her shoulder. Thankful for the small gesture of comfort, Dorie nodded and stepped away from his touch. "Thank you for preparing the fire. I shall begin breakfast shortly. I wish to speak to Hannah first."

"Take all the time you need. I'll start breakfast."

Dorie came to a standstill in the doorway. She looked as if she had been carved in marble. Turning, she said, "You? Cook?"

He smiled. "Can't be that difficult to cook a few eggs. Slice some bread. Anything else you would like me to prepare."

Dorie stood in the door and chewed on her bottom lip. "I don't mean to sound ungrateful, but that idea has disaster written all over it."

He crossed his arms over his chest. "And what makes you think I can't cook?" he demanded.

"I . . . you . . ." She inhaled deeply. "Ash, you have the hands of a gentleman."

Ash looked at his hands and shrugged. "So? Doesn't mean I cannot cook breakfast."

"But will it be edible?" she asked.

"Of course," he said, even though he possessed little confidence.

"If you'll wait until I return, we shall cook breakfast together." With the statement still floating in the air, Dorie departed.

Ash stared after her. He would show her he was quite capable of cooking breakfast if it was the last thing he did.

"What are you doing?" the soft voice whispered behind Ash.

He turned and smiled. "Good morning, Mrs. Dorrington. I'm cooking breakfast."

Her eyes widened. "Dorie is allowing you to cook?" she asked in obvious surprise.

Ash nodded, feeling no need to divulge the truth.

"She never permits me to cook," she confided. "And call me Rose."

Ash nodded and asked, "Would you like to assist me?" He could probably use all the assistance he could get.

A smile appeared and joy sheathed her face. "Oh, yes. I was once a splendid cook."

"Well, by all means, your assistance is welcome." Picking up the apron he had planned to use himself, he said, "Here's an apron to protect your dress." Rose stood perfectly still as Ash tied it around her waist.

"I was just examining the contents of the larder. What do you usually have for breakfast?"

"Porridge."

A GIFT OF LOVE

He waited for her to continue, but nothing more was forthcoming. "Is that all?"

"And tea."

"Nothing else?"

She shook her head.

Ash drummed his fingers on his chin. What in the devil was in porridge? Best to ask and not create a disaster. "How does one make porridge?"

"You cook the oats in water and when they are done, you add cream and honey."

That sounded reasonable to him.

Ash dipped water from the bucket and poured it into a pot. He dumped oats into the water and stirred it.

"You need to put more oats," Rose advised.

Ash looked at Rose carefully. She must know the way of it. After all, she was a female. All females knew how to cook. Didn't they?

He poured more oats into the pot, and then lit the wood in the stove. At least they did not cook over an open fire. Setting the pot on the stove, he gave it another good stir. He picked up the bag and oats dusted the floor. Ash shrugged, content to let the cleanup wait.

"I think we should have more than porridge. I noticed some eggs in the larder. Scones would be good, but I have no idea how to make them. You?"

Rose shook her head.

"Eggs and toast sound good." He looked at Rose, his brow raised in question.

She nodded. "Yes, Ash, but I don't know if we should use Dorie's eggs."

"I'm sure she will not mind." Ash's brow furrowed. "How does one make toast?"

"You slice bread and place it in the toaster. Then, place the toaster over the fire."

"Shall I do that and you cook the eggs?"

Rose chewed on her lower lip. "Very well."

Ash began to slice the bread. A muttered "Oh, dear" and a splat broke through his concentration. Without looking up, he asked, "Is something wrong, Rose?"

"I-I seem to have broken the egg wrong."

"There is a right way?" Ash asked, stupefied.

"The wrong side," she explained.

"There is a right side to crack it?"

"The wrong side of the bowl," she huffed.

He eyed the shattered egg lying on the table. Yellow and white blurred together amidst the remnants of the shell. Ash shrugged. "Don't overly concern yourself, madam. Accidents are bound to happen," he consoled, and went back to slicing the bread.

Pain sliced through Ash's thumb. "Bloody hell." All he saw was the obscene bright red blood oozing into the bread.

Rose muttered, "Oh, dear! You have cut your thumb."

Ash was surprised Rose could move so quickly. She dipped a rag into the water and wrapped it around his thumb. "Dorie must put some of her salve on it. You mustn't let it get infected."

Ash nodded and quiet settled over the kitchen except for the crackle of the fire and the tap of the knife on the wooden table. Cooking was fairly easy. He must have cooked before. He began whistling a jaunty tune.

Ash finished slicing the bread and asked, "Where is the toaster?"

Rose still stood at the table wringing her hands, worry furrowing her brow. She pointed to the larder. After a successful search, he placed the toaster on the table and began sliding the bread slices between the bars.

He gazed from the fireplace to the oven and shrugged. He placed the bread over the open flame and turned back to Rose. "I'll crack the eggs now."

He lightly tapped the egg on the bowl and opened it. A huge hunk of shell dropped into the bowl. "Bloody hell," he cursed and spooned the shell out. Rose stood beside him, wringing her hands and muttering under her breath, "Dorie will murder us."

"Nonsense. She shall be appreciative of our assistance," Ash stated with little confidence as he gently cracked another egg on the bowl's edge.

A quick intake of breath sounded from the door. "What have you done to my kitchen?" Dorie questioned.

Ash looked up and smiled, confident she would be greatly pleased. "Rose and I are cooking breakfast."

His smile slowly dissolved as her fury registered in the back of his mind. The morning sunlight accentuated the anger glittering in her blue eyes and setting her pink lips in a tight, grim line. Perhaps Rose had been right. With both hands on her hips, Dorie looked ready to murder him. "Is there a problem?" he drawled, pushing his annoyance away. She should be grateful for his assistance.

"You have never cooked," she charged, and stalked over to him.

He did not retreat under her advance. "I'm not sure if I have or not."

"Believe me, I can tell you have not. What ever possessed you? And you used my eggs!" she cried in dismay.

The tips of his ears burned. He would not allow this thankless chit to embarrass him. Through gritted teeth he said, "Trying to help you, but I see my assistance is unwanted. You are an ungrateful baggage."

Dorie leaned her head back and gazed into his eyes. "I do not appreciate people in my kitchen."

A loud *plop* filled the room. Everyone turned just as the porridge oozed over the side of the pot and ran down to slather the stove.

A nervous twitter interrupted them. "Dorie, can you not chastise us later? We have a problem with the toast."

Dorie sighed and swung around to face Rose. Black smoke billowed from the fireplace. Ash pushed Dorie out of harm's way and grabbed the toaster handle. It clattered on the floor as he cursed, "Bloody damn hell!" and shook his hand.

Dorie grabbed his arm and pulled him over to the water bucket. She plunged his hand into the cold water and ordered, "Leave it."

Rose grabbed up a cloth, intent on picking up the toaster, but Dorie laid a gentle hand on her arm and took the cloth away. "Please sit down, Aunt Rose. I shall handle this calamity."

Rose nodded.

Ash drew his hand up to look at the burn and Dorie ordered, "Put it back in the water."

He looked over and she glared at him. He resub-

A GIFT OF LOVE 47

merged his hand as Dorie picked up the toaster. The bread was as black as a pot, and she unceremoniously dumped the overcrisp toast onto the garbage.

Then she picked up the pot and peered inside. "What is this supposed to be?" Thick gray mush drizzled to the floor.

"Porridge."

Dorie rolled her eyes as the muck accompanied the toast onto the garbage pile.

"Was that really necessary?" Ash inquired.

"It is exactly where it belongs," Dorie informed him, and grabbed a potato.

"I shall wipe up the porridge," Ash said.

"You shall rest your burned hand."

Ash eyed her as she deftly peeled the potato and minced it. Finally, he could not control his curiosity. "What the devil are you doing?"

"The potato will relieve the pain and swelling of the burn."

Ash's brow furrowed. "I have never heard of such a treatment."

Dorie shrugged. "It is an old country remedy my grandmother taught me. She was a great believer in using herbs and other vegetation."

Dorie gently laid Ash's hand on the cloth. White blisters were raised across his fingers. She covered the burn with the chopped potato.

Her hands were cool and delicate upon his hand. As gentle as an angel. He inhaled deeply to fight the gnawing awareness and the fragrance of roses filled his head. How did she manage to smell of roses in the winter?

As Dorie leaned over his hand, Ash was free to study her. Once again her thick mahogany hair was pinned back in a severe chignon. But her blue dress, faded and worn, hugged her body in a most pleasant way.

His body hardened in reaction to her. Ash closed his eyes and ordered the thoughts away. He did not even know who he was. He must remain immune to her. He could not afford any emotional entanglements.

Miss Dorie Knighton was not his type of woman. He hesitated. How did he know what his type of woman was? Well, one thing was certain. Dorie was not his type, whatever his type was.

Five

"All of our Christmas guests have arrived except Ash. Thor, isn't it time to send the footmen searching for him? Even Pemberton is worried."

Drake Stanton, the Earl of Thorley, looked up from his ledger and leaned back into the leather chair. He smiled at his wife.

Bella was even more beautiful than four years ago when he'd married her. A glow of expectant motherhood radiated from her emerald eyes.

"Ash's valet is a mother hen. I'm sure Ash is good and well."

Bella kissed Thor's cheek and perched on the edge of the desk. She smoothed her silk gown. "Just why did he send Pemberton on ahead?" Bella asked with narrowed eyes.

Thor shifted his gaze to the window. "He had business to attend to."

"Darling, you have never been able to lie to me. It was a woman, wasn't it?"

Thor's gaze returned to Bella and he sighed heavily. She was right. He could never lie to her. There was no point in whitewashing the matter. "Yes. He served his latest mistress with her congé."

"And why did he get rid of this one?"

"She had an indiscretion with another man."

Bella gritted her teeth. "Of course, he can have as many women as he likes. He is such a rogue. He needs to settle down and marry. Concentrate his attention on a wife and children and his estate rather than bedding every willing woman."

Thor kissed Bella's hand. "He just hasn't met the right woman yet."

"I sometimes wonder if he would recognize her if he did meet his true soul mate."

"Now, Bella, Ash is not dense. He'll recognize her and she shall be lucky. After all, rakes in love make the best husbands."

Bella smiled warmly and caressed his cheek. "Yes, they most certainly do."

Thor stared into her emerald eyes for a moment, glad to have made this wonderful woman his wife and the mother of his future children. Never once did he miss the old days of carousing.

Bella sighed. "I really should leave you to your work. By the way, do you know where your grandmother's silver teapot is?"

Thor's eyebrow rose in surprise, but he shook his head. "I'm certain the servants know. You usually don't bother me with household matters."

"I've asked everyone else. No one remembers seeing it the last two days. As if the teapot disappeared into thin air."

"I'm sure one of the servants will find it. None of our servants or guests would steal anything," he said with confidence.

A high-pitched scream pierced the air. Bella rolled her eyes. "What now?"

Thor sighed. "I suppose I should go discover what the ruckus is."

The door opened and the butler entered. "Sorry for the disturbance, my lord and lady."

"What seems to be the problem, Barrett?"

"Mrs. Dorrington was visiting again. She walked in on Lady Marwood and gave her a fright. I've instructed a footman to walk Mrs. Dorrington home."

"Thank you," Thor said.

When Barrett had exited, Bella sighed heavily and said, "I shall have to inform Mama not to fret. It's a shame that Dorie's aunt gets lost and can't remember her way home."

Thor agreed. "I'm afraid she'll hurt herself one day."

Bella caressed his cheek once again and smiled. "Until later, darling."

Thor stared after her as she strolled out and watched her hips swish from side to side. He felt his body react to the stimulating sight and sighed. He would have to wait until they retired for the evening. Houseguests were quite irritating at times.

Bright sunlight reflected off the pristine snow that covered her small lawn. Dorie smiled as she and Hannah rolled snow into a large ball. Come spring, red and yellow flowers would dot the yard and pink roses would cover the bush climbing the wall.

Hannah patted the ball and pronounced, "This is going to be a wonderful snowman. Did you find everything we need in Papa's belongings?"

Dorie dusted the snow off her gloves and answered, "I certainly did." She glanced at the window.

Rose watched them from the warmth of the cottage. Rose fluttered her fingers at her. Dorie smiled and returned the wave.

Hannah's muffled voice filtered through her scarf. "When we finish the snowman, may we make Christmas angels?"

Dorie bent to assist making the second ball and said, "If we are not frozen."

A deep voice broke from the walkway. "What's this? Two Christmas angels making huge snowballs?"

Hannah giggled. "Not at all, Ash. We are building a snowman."

"I see. Then may I be of assistance?"

Dorie asked, "Are you any better at making snowmen than you are at cooking?"

The tips of Ash's ears turned bright red. It must be the cold. Her words could not have embarrassed him, could they?

Ash's eyes twinkled as he replied with a serious mien, "Of course. Boys are always quite clever at building snowmen."

Dorie snorted, but said nothing as Ash rolled snow into a ball for the head.

Flattening the rounded tops to sit securely, Ash stacked the three balls of snow on top of each other from largest to smallest. "Do you have materials for his face?"

Hannah answered, "Yes." She pressed two lumps of coal into the snow for eyes, a carrot for his nose, and several small pebbles into a spectral grin.

Ash said, "I believe his nose is a little long. May I?"

Hannah nodded.

Ash broke part of the carrot off and pressed it into the snowman's face again.

Hannah giggled and clapped her hands. "Much better." She then stuck a pipe into his grinning mouth, a beaver hat on his head, and a scarf around his neck.

Tilting her head, Dorie said, "He needs some arms."

"We can remedy that."

As Ash snapped two limbs off a tree, Dorie contemplated him. He displayed no trouble reaching the limbs or in neatly breaking them off. His greatcoat strained across his wide shoulders. Shoulders strong enough to bear heavy burdens without bending.

He strolled back and stuck the limbs into the snowman, making a set of spindly arms.

Hannah laughed with glee. "He is wonderful."

The words startled Dorie, who for a moment was not certain if Hannah spoke of Ash or the snowman. But Hannah's eyes were focused on the snowman.

Ash whispered from behind Dorie, "I believe she is talking about the snowman."

Dorie whirled around, convinced for the moment that Ash had read her mind. His eyes twinkled with amusement. "I momentarily thought she spoke of my being wonderful."

"I believe Hannah does think you are wonderful also." Dorie turned back to watch Hannah.

Ash stepped closer, his coat brushing her shoulder. "Too bad her sister does not surmise so. I sadly humiliated myself with my breakfast assistance. I shall never be forgiven."

Ash's dark eyes bored into her. She no longer felt

the cold. Instead, the heat of a thousand suns burned within her. "Never is a long time." Her stomach clenched with a foreign sensation. She was too aware of his nearness, of his exhilarating male scent. A sense of vertigo threatened her equilibrium.

"True. I wonder what it would take to get back in her good graces."

Dorie inhaled deeply and squeezed her eyes tight. The urge to turn and cling to him infused her being. To bury her face in his chest and feel his strong arms around her, his warm lips covering hers with passion. What would it be like for Ash to make love to her? To possess her in a way she had never allowed a man to do before?

Her curiosity about Ash was dangerous. That thought had come freely and without hindrance. Ash would not stay here forever, no matter how much she might want him to. Soon, his memory would return, and with it his life. For all they knew, he was married.

These thoughts and feelings were confusing and astonishing. She had only known Ash for a few days, and would never have believed such intense emotions were possible after such a short time. Nothing in her life had prepared her for this startling reaction.

"Dorie, what is wrong?" His hands clasped her shoulders and turned her to him.

The warm concern in his voice was almost her undoing. Dorie opened her eyes and forced a smile. "I'm sorry. I-I guess I was daydreaming."

"About what?"

She forced herself to smile brighter. "Nothing of

import. I believe you were speaking of getting back in someone's good graces."

His gloved finger brushed her cheek. "Are you certain you are well? You are very pale."

She nodded and stepped away from him.

Something flickered in the depths of Ash's eyes for a fleeting moment before he covered it with amusement. Dorie almost believed it was disappointment, but that was utterly ridiculous.

She coerced a lightness from the depths of her soul. "Hannah, are you ready to make snow angels?"

Hannah dashed over to them and clapped her hands. "Yes, yes, yes."

"Pray tell, how does one make snow angels?"

Hannah turned disbelieving eyes on Ash. "You have never made snow angels?"

He smiled and chucked Hannah's chin. "Not that I recall, but I know you shall be adept in showing me how."

Hannah promptly lay in the snow and fluttered her arms and legs.

"You aren't worried about her catching the ague?" he whispered.

"Of course, but I cannot encase her in glass and sit her on a shelf, no matter how much I might wish to. It takes so very little to make her happy. Building a snowman and making snow angels are the least I can allow her. But when we go inside, she takes a bath and drinks plenty of hot tea."

"And what will it take to make *you* happy?"

Dorie jerked her gaze away from Hannah to Ash's smoldering dark eyes. "I am happy."

"I have not heard you laugh."

"One does not have to laugh to be happy."

He arched a brow in disbelief. "No?"

"No," she insisted.

"It seems to me that if a person enjoyed life, there would be laughter."

"Maybe to the frivolous people of the world."

"You think laughter is frivolous?"

Had she really said such a thing? It sounded ridiculous to her own ears, but she refused to back down under his intense gaze. It was not that she did not enjoy laughter, but her responsibilities left little time for laughter or joy.

"So many concern themselves only with shallow enjoyments, never thinking of the less fortunate."

Ash opened his mouth to reply, but before he could utter a sound, a snowball hit him full in the mouth.

Dorie's mouth gaped in shock. "Hannah!"

Hannah only giggled and in a singsong voice said, "I got Ash! I got Ash!"

Dorie brushed snow from his shoulder and asked, "Are you all right?"

The urge to laugh bubbled up from inside her. Dorie chewed her bottom lip, trying to halt the laughter. She could not very well laugh in his face.

Ash spit snow from his mouth and bestowed her with a mock glare. "You think that was funny?"

Dorie shook her head, unable to trust herself to answer him with a straight face.

"Then why are you having so much difficulty controlling your laughter?" Without waiting for her reply, Ash bent over and scooped up two handfuls of snow. He began to shape them into a ball.

Dorie backed away, never taking her eyes off his

busy hands. She shook her head and contended, "You wouldn't!"

He grinned and waggled his brows, his eyes full of devilment. "Think so?"

Before she could turn and run from his intent, a snowball hit her square in the chest. Dorie's mouth gaped open. "You scoundrel! Hannah threw it, not me."

"Yes, but you laughed. But I shall also repay Hannah." Once again, Ash scooped up snow, pressed it together, and aimed at Hannah.

Hannah screamed and ducked. The snowball flew over her head. Jumping up, she laughed and danced around. "Missed me! Missed me!"

Dorie served up her own snowball, hitting Ash square in the mouth. His gloved hand brushed the snow from his pink face and said, "Very well, ladies, you fired the first shots. Now it is all-out war."

Snowballs flew fast and furious. Some found their mark, others missed. But beneath all the hubbub clamored laughter and joy.

Dorie was shocked at herself, for it seemed ages since she had laughed and given herself up to the enjoyment of a moment. But on this winter morning, even though she was cold and wet, she was having a grand time. So much so, her face hurt from laughing. For the moment, worry was far from her mind.

While Ash's attention was on fighting off Hannah's snowballs, Dorie crept behind him and slipped snow inside his coat.

Ash bellowed a war cry and Dorie quickly retreated. He turned and charged Dorie, leaving her no time to escape. His body crashed into her, bringing her down. The snow softened their fall.

Dorie could not breathe. It was as if a stone wall had fallen on her. Ash's body was hard and unyielding. He raised his head and stared at her mouth. His eyes seemed to grow even blacker and a fire kindled within their depths. His head slowly lowered.

Good Lord! He is going to kiss me! Her pulse pounded and her mouth suddenly felt as dry as a desert. Dorie turned her head to the side and his kiss landed on her cheek. Her face flamed with embarrassment.

He stilled for a moment, then heaved a great sigh. "I beg your pardon, Dorie. I do not know what possessed me to do such a thing."

Dorie simply nodded, unsure of her ability to keep her voice steady.

Ash came to his feet and held his hand out. Dorie hesitated a moment, then put her hand in his. His large hand swallowed hers as he helped her to her feet.

Gone was the camaraderie of moments ago. In its place lay uneasiness as heavy as a woolen blanket. Dorie admitted to herself the reason for her discomfort. The feel of Ash had been delightful, warm and solid.

Hannah dashed up, breaking her thoughts. "Dorie, are you well?"

She forced a smile for her little sister. "Yes, I'm fine. Do not fret over me."

"Your sister has forgiven me for my clumsiness." Ash reached out and laid his hand on Hannah's cheek.

Hannah gazed from Ash to Dorie and back again. Dorie identified the ambivalence in her eyes. Hannah was not certain what had transpired, but she did not believe that it was simply clumsiness on Ash's part.

Dorie whirled around to look at the window. She relaxed. Aunt Rose was not there to have seen the kiss.

Dorie bit back a sigh of relief. She could be thankful for that small miracle.

The sound of splashing water filtered through the thin wall for what seemed like the hundredth time. Ash gritted his teeth and breathed deeply. He had never realized simple sounds could be so erotic, and he still remembered how Dorie had felt beneath him that afternoon. Soft and warm, smelling like roses. And her lips would have tasted as sweet as honey, if only she had not turned her head.

He closed his eyes and an image loomed before him of Dorie standing in the tub. Milk white skin as smooth as silk. High-perched breasts that would just fill his hand and luscious raspberry nipples that would taste sweet and ripe in his mouth. A slim waist that his hands would encircle to lower her down. Legs, long and smooth, to wrap around his waist while he made her his.

Ash groaned and turned his face into the goose down pillow. He would soon be a madman at this rate. Forcing his mind to concentrate, Ash tried to relax the hard throbbing in certain portions of his anatomy.

Hannah had been first to bathe after they returned from their outside romp. Dorie was now bathing, and his imagination was working overtime. He was supposed to be next, but he really needed a dunking in cold water to alleviate his problem.

He endeavored to think of something other than the erotic scene occurring just on the other side of the wall. He felt like Hercules straining to meet one of his tasks.

A soft sigh of pleasure sifted through the wall. He wished he had been the cause of her pleasure. *Bloody hell!* Unable to sit still any longer, Ash jumped up and paced to the fireplace. *What the devil was the woman doing?*

He paced back across the room. Did she always enjoy a bath so? He was struck by an urge so strong he had to grasp the mantle to restrain himself. He wanted to rush next door, strip his own clothes off, and leap into the tub with her.

He admitted he was driving himself insane with his licentious thoughts, but his mind seemed to be stuck in this living nightmare.

A portion of his brain said, *Forget everything but seducing her.* It was as if the devil sat on his shoulder.

The conscientious part replied, *But I may be married.*

So, what does that matter? That does not hinder you from making love to any number of women, and this one is a sweet morsel.

It's not right to take advantage.

But she wants you to. I've seen the way she looks at you.

She does not look at me in that way.

Of course she does.

Ridiculous. She is a proper young lady.

The devil snorted. *Who wants you to ruin her. Just think what it would be like to sink into her damp heat.*

"Go away!" Ash shouted. He stilled, barely able to breathe. Had he shouted out loud?

Dorie's soft voice filtered through to his ear. "Ash? Is something wrong?"

The tips of his ears burned. "No. I had just fallen asleep and was having a nightmare," he lied.

"I shall be finished shortly. Then we'll refill the tub for you."

"Very well," he managed to mumble. *Damnation, it was going to be a long night.*

Six

Dorie sat by the fire knitting. The blaze was warm and crisp on her face. Hannah had gone to bed immediately after supper, worn out by the snowball fight. She had even asked Ash to tuck her in.

"May I join you?"

The deep voice caused her breath to catch in her throat. "Please do." She forced the words out.

Ash settled in the chair next to her and stuck his legs straight out, one ankle crossed over the other.

"Hannah is all tucked in," he murmured.

"It took a long time."

"She asked me to tell her a story."

"It is kind of you to please her, but you must not let her take advantage."

"Not at all. Actually, I enjoyed it."

"Did it seem a familiar ritual?"

His brows rose in question. "What?"

"I thought maybe you have children of your own and it would seem familiar."

"Not a bit. Though I cannot deny it would be nice to have children." Ash sighed. "At times I wonder if I will ever regain my memory."

Dorie laid her hand lightly on Ash's arm. She

tried desperately to ignore the heat scorching her through his clothes. "You must be patient. I am certain your memory will return in time."

Ash sighed again. "I wish I believed."

"It has only been three days. You must practice patience."

Ash nodded and said, "Yes, I know, even though that task is difficult, I suppose I have no other choice."

The next day Ash accompanied Dorie into the village. It had been three days since his accident, and he still remembered nothing.

The sleepy hamlet of gray stone was built around a green now layered in snow; the stream was a ribbon of ice. At one end, was a church with a low Norman tower mellowed by weather and time. Obviously, a village of some age and history.

They entered the village shop, apparently the place to purchase whatever one needed. Ash roamed around, looking at all the essential items the establishment contained. Needles and thread. Boots and bootlaces. Bolts of fabric as well as buttons and lace. Cooking pans and teapots.

But the visit to the shop produced no enlightening flashes. Charming and picturesque, the village brought no memories forth. Disappointment permeated Ash. He had hoped he would remember previous visits to the village, or that someone might recognize him.

Dorie talked quietly to the proprietor. Ash smoothed his hand over a bolt of blue woolen cloth and wished he possessed enough coin to have coats fashioned for Dorie and Hannah.

Stopping at a display of knitted items, Ash studied the scarves, gloves, and tea cozies. Dorie had spent many hours making these items. He picked up a scarf and studied the closely knitted yarn.

Ash turned his attention to Dorie, her face pale and strained in the bright morning light. Highlights of burnished mahogany shimmered in her deep brown hair, once again pulled into a severe chignon. But wisps of hair had worked free and framed her heart-shaped face.

A soul forged in fire. She was a woman a man could trust and depend upon. He doubted he would ever find Miss Pandora Knighton breaking vows or even swooning.

He threw the scarf down in disgust. Standing in a tacky shop mooning over a woman. He was getting as sappy as a lovesick poet.

"Ash!"

He turned to find large emerald eyes glaring at him. Ash gaped at the woman a moment, a surge of disbelief and exhilaration rising. A rush of recollection flowed through him as if his entire life was unfolding before his eyes.

A smile tugged at his lips; finally, gaining momentum, it covered his face. He bowed and kissed her hand. "Good morning, Bella. You're looking very lovely today."

"You rascal!" she exclaimed. "We have been worried sick over you and here you are *shopping*. Not that I would have thought you would set foot in a small village shop such as this."

Ash opened his mouth, but no sound was forthcoming. He looked around and his gaze fell on Dorie. She stood next to him, staring at him in wide-eyed disbelief. Laughter floated up from his throat, triumphant and exuberant.

His hands encircled her waist and twirled her around. "I'm Nathan Langford, Marquess of Ashborne! I came to Yorkshire to spend Christmas with Bella and Thor, my best friend. I cannot believe my memory flooded back all at once."

Dorie's fingers dug into his shoulders as she clung to him. He heard her quick intake of air.

"Put poor Dorie down before you make her sick," Bella chastised. "She is beginning to look green."

Ash set Dorie on her feet, but still her hands clung to him as she tried to regain her equilibrium.

"I-I'm happy you have your memory back, my lord," Dorie whispered, and stared at the floor.

Putting a finger under her chin, Ash raised her face to look at him. She smiled tentatively.

"No 'my lords' between us, Dorie. I appreciate everything you have done for me. I would like to repay you."

Dorie's shoulders straightened and her hands dropped to her sides. She jerked her chin away from his finger. "That is not necessary. I do not need charity."

Ash winced. She made *charity* sound like a foul word. "It would not be charity. After all, you took me in and fed me and warmed me for three days."

Bella's brows rose in question and Ash sighed. She had been silently watching him and Dorie. Ash believed there was a glint of speculation in her eye. He touched the bruise on his head and explained,

"I've had amnesia for three days from this knock on the head. Dorie found me and saved my life."

Bella's mouth gaped in shock. "Are you serious?"

Ash nodded.

"You poor dear." Bella turned to Dorie and said, "Good morning. I hope Hannah and Mrs. Dorrington are well."

Dorie affected a neat curtsy. "Very well. Thank you, Lady Thorley."

Bella turned to Ash. "Shall we expect you later today?"

Ash nodded. "I'll accompany Dorie home after she completes her shopping. I do not know what happened to my horse. Will you send a carriage to retrieve me?"

"Of course, Ash." Bella eyed the white bandage over one hand. "What happened?"

Ash smiled sheepishly and muttered, "I attempted to cook breakfast." He held up the bandaged hand. "As you can see, I was a dismal failure."

Bella's eyes widened in surprise. "You must be funning me! The Marquess of Ashborne *cooking?*"

" 'Tis true. Dorie will confirm it."

Bella looked at Dorie. She nodded in confirmation.

Bella shook her head. "Dorie, I hope to see you tomorrow afternoon when the village ladies meet to prepare the baskets for the poor."

Dorie smiled. "Yes. Aunt Rose wishes to come with me."

"By all means, bring Mrs. Dorrington and Hannah. I hope you will stay for dinner."

Indecision etched Dorie's face. Ash was certain she was about to refuse the invitation when Bella

A GIFT OF LOVE 67

said, "Thor expressed a desire to see Hannah." Bella patted her rounded stomach and laughed. "I believe he wants to practice fatherhood."

"How is Thor's heir? I am amazed he allowed you out." Ash chuckled. "I have never seen a man so nervous."

Bella raised her chin. "Heir, indeed! All you men think alike. I may just decide to have a daughter."

Ash laughed and hugged her. "You would do it just to spite Thor. My felicitations."

"Thank you, Ash. Now, we just have to find a wife for you so you can have a child."

Ash frowned and stepped back. "Quit trying to marry me off, Bella. It's not a very becoming trait for a lady."

Bella rolled her eyes and laughed. "I shall never rest until you are reformed." She patted Ash's arm. "Farewell, Dorie."

"Good-bye, Lady Thorley."

Ash turned back to Dorie. "It is lucky I came to the village today. Seeing Bella triggered my memory."

Dorie nodded quietly. "I will not take me long to finish my shopping."

"Take your time." He stared after Dorie as she walked across the shop. For some odd reason, he did not really feel lucky. He should be bursting with joy to have his memory back, but instead he felt strangely hollow.

"I don't see why Ash had to leave us," Hannah complained.

If the child said it one more time, Dorie would

scream. But that was being unfair. Hannah was heartbroken.

"There was no need for him to stay. He has his memory back and his friends were expecting him for Christmas. And he is a marquess, Hannah. When you see him tomorrow, you must remember to call him 'my lord'."

Hannah's bottom lip protruded. "I don't want him to be a lord."

Dorie smiled at Hannah. "Well, he is and there is nothing to be done about it. I imagine he is quite happy to be out of our meager cottage."

Hannah looked around. "What's wrong with our cottage?"

"He is accustomed to more affluent surroundings. You remember Lord Thorley's house?"

She nodded. "It's gigantic and beautiful."

"Yes, not a threadbare chair in sight, nor wormy wood."

Hannah sighed. "Someday I'll live in a house like that."

"Houses and material things are not important," Dorie gently chided. "Honesty, truth, and kindness are the important things."

"But can't you have those things and still live in a nice house?"

Dorie hesitated. How did one explain to a child? "It is not impossible. A lot of people have lives worse than ours. We have a dry, warm cottage and enough to eat. Many go hungry and have no roof over their heads."

Hannah seemed to think about that a moment, then said, "I'll take the nice house."

Dorie smiled. "We do not always get to choose

our lot in life, Hannah. If we did, everyone would live in a nice house."

"My angel will provide for us. Just you wait and see." Hannah jumped up and kissed Dorie's cheek. "Good night."

"Sweet dreams." Dorie laid her knitting in her lap and stared into the crackling fire. She hated to see Hannah disappointed.

Dinner had been a dismal affair this evening. Hannah had begged Ash to stay. He had just smiled and said he could not; he must join his friends.

Ash had said all the right things. Thanked them profusely for their assistance. But Dorie had a suspicion he was glad to be away from their genteel poverty. Her small, inferior cottage and plain food had been quite a step down for a marquess.

Dorie's heart thudded as a thought entered her head. She just might see Ash tomorrow when they assembled food baskets for the poor. A cynical voice cut through her mind: *And what does it matter if you do see him? He's a peer and you a poor schoolmaster's daughter. Far above your reach.*

She scolded her inner voice, *Do not be ridiculous. I have never thought of him in that way. He is a friend. Nothing more.*

A soft voice broke through her reverie. "Dorie?"

She shook herself and turned to Rose. "Yes, Aunt?"

"Where is your husband?"

What in the devil was she talking about? Dorie squeezed Rose's hand. "I have no husband, Aunt."

Rose looked at her, confusion clouding her face. "Of course you do," Rose insisted. "I saw him in your bedchamber."

"No, Aunt Rose. That was Ash. I found him injured in the snow and he stayed with us three days."

"You're not married?"

Dorie shook her head.

"Then he must marry you. He has compromised you!"

"No, Aunt. We were never alone," she fibbed. "You and Hannah chaperoned me."

"We did?"

Dorie nodded.

"Well, I suppose it is all right, then."

Dorie closed her eyes and prayed Aunt Rose would not say anything unseemly at Lord and Lady Thorley's tomorrow. Maybe Dorie could at least keep her reputation intact.

A shiver came over Dorie as if someone watched her. She twisted around to find a ghostlike figure hovering in the doorway.

Seven

The gown billowed around Hannah like a shroud, and her hair hung loose around her face, but it did not conceal the look of wonder and awe.

"What is it?" Dorie asked. "Are you ill?"

Strolling toward her, Hannah never raised her gaze from her outstretched hand. "I-I found it in Ash's bed."

Dorie dropped her gaze to find a feather. The fear and horror inside her loosened. "It is only a goose feather from the mattress."

Hannah shook her head. "It's from his angel's wings."

Dorie's mouth gaped open in astonishment. She forced her mouth closed and took a deep breath. She must handle this without harming Hannah's feelings. "Dear heart, Ash is not an angel. He is merely a man with all the flaws of a mortal."

Hannah disagreed. "No, Dorie. He really is my angel. Being human, we cannot see his wings."

"He is as human as we are. We have proof that he bleeds just like us."

Hannah's fingers folded and enveloped the ordinary feather. "I believe," she whispered, and scampered off.

Dorie stared after her, and then squeezed her eyes shut. Heartbreak was ahead for Hannah, and she was powerless to halt it.

Ash stared into the crackling fire and sipped a snifter of brandy. Dinner had been a long, tiresome affair. So different from the Knightons' family meals.

"Am I interrupting?"

Ash turned and smiled at Thor. "Not at all. I was just enjoying a glass of your fine brandy before bed."

"If you do not mind, I shall join you."

"Not at all."

Thor settled into the chair next to Ash. "Is anything wrong? You're not quite your old self tonight."

"No. I imagine I'm just tired and worn out from my ordeal. I shall recover in a day or two."

Thor swirled his brandy. "Does your hand pain you? I doubt your head does. It is too hard to damage."

Ash laughed and shook his head.

Thor said, "Am I to understand you burned your hand *cooking*?"

"Yes." Ash glared at Thor. "You shall badger me about that forever."

Thor threw back his head and laughed. "Indeed." Thor sobered and asked, "What did you think of the Misses Knighton and Mrs. Dorrington?"

Ash hesitated, choosing his words carefully. "They are most kind. Not many would take a stranger into their home and care for him."

"True. Miss Dorie is an unusual young woman."

"I discovered she hates anything smacking of charity. I wish I could repay her kindness. They need so much."

"Some would say they are richer than most," Thor commented.

Ash shrugged.

Thor asked, "Do you remember what caused you to fall off your horse?"

"No. That is the one thing I've yet to recall."

"Perhaps you should have sidestepped your last rendezvous. If you had traveled with Pemberton, you would have avoided your mishap."

Ash rubbed his chin. "I doubt it."

"Do not tell me you believe in fate," Thor said, incredulousness evident in his voice.

"No." Ash grinned and changed the subject. "So, how fares the father-to-be?"

A smile broke across Thor's face and his eyes glowed with joy. "Wonderful. Can't wait to hold him."

Ash's grin grew bigger. "Bella informs me she may decide to have a girl. She does not like the assumption that it will be your heir."

Thor laughed. "Yes, I know. I cannot tell you how many times I have heard that particular remark. But a daughter will suit me well also." Thor then growled, "I shall just have to keep her away from the likes of you."

"The likes of me?" Ash managed to look hurt. "I'm titled and wealthy. What more could you want?"

"Someone who is not a salacious rake."

"Ah, but it is said rakes make the best husbands."

"Yes, *if* they fall in love. Bella can claim proof of that."

Ash snorted and almost choked on his brandy. "Modest as ever, I see."

Thor shrugged. "So, what do you plan to do about assisting the Knightons?"

Ash cursed to himself. That was the last subject he wanted to talk about. Apparently, Thor would not be put off. "Nothing. I shall go on my merry way and forget them."

"Very callous of you."

Ash shrugged. "What would you have me do? Miss Knighton is quite adamant about accepting anything akin to charity."

"You are smart enough to think of a way to repay her without her knowing exactly where it comes from."

Ash stared into the fire. His finger circled the rim of the crystal snifter. "You think so?"

"Yes. You manage not to get caught as you tiptoe from one woman's bed to another. At least you never meddle with innocent young girls." His voice was hard and full of censure.

"You sound so disapproving. No one would ever guess you were exactly the same until you married."

Thor frowned.

Ash laughed and continued, "I know, I know. You do not like to be reminded of your days before Bella." He leaned back into the leather chair, propped his ankle on his knee, and drummed his fingers. Staring into the fire, he contemplated if he should find a way to repay Dorie Knighton.

Eight

The next day dawned cold and dreary. *Just like my mood*, Dorie thought. Hannah had been desolate since Ash's departure, which had dampened her spirits like nothing before.

Hannah and Aunt Rose joined her in the cart as she set off for Thorley Park. It was an annual event to prepare baskets for the poor of their village. At one time the other women had attempted to give her a basket, but she quickly told them she was not in need of their charity.

After all, her means were more substantial than those of many people. Her father had left her a nice cottage with no holes in the roof or the walls. They never went hungry and they had plenty of heat in the winter.

"Dorie, will Ash be at Thorley Park?" Hannah asked.

"I'm not certain. I suppose it is possible. If he is, you must remember to address him as 'my lord'."

Hannah scrunched up her nose at Dorie's counsel. "Why? We know him well."

"We did not know he was a peer when he stayed with us. However, we now know he is the Marquess of Ashborne. As such, we must give him the proper respect and not be overly familiar."

"Ash doesn't want that. He liked us."

"Still, we are not on the same social level with him."

"Is he the young man who was in your bed?" Rose asked.

Dorie groaned. "Yes, Aunt Rose, but you must not say such a thing in front of anyone."

Rose's brow knitted. "If you wish, I'll try, but sometimes I cannot help myself. I-I'm sorry, Dorie." She stared at her clasped hands twisting in her lap. "It must be very difficult to love me."

Dorie squeezed Rose's hand. "Not at all. I love you very much, Aunt Rose. I do not know what Hannah and I would do without you."

Rose smiled. "That is nice, my dear. Thank you. I love you and Hannah very much also. Things just have not been the same since my dear husband died, and then your father." Rose shook her head and clucked her tongue. "So sad."

Booms reverberated in the distance. Rose jumped. "W-what was that?"

Dorie patted her hand. "Must be a shooting party from Thorley House."

"Poor birds," Hannah said. "Why must they shoot the pretty birds?"

"It is now the season for partridge and pheasant. Lord Thorley does not allow the killing of more than is needed to grace his dinner table. Many slaughter simply for the kill."

Dorie turned her pony into the Thorley Park drive, passing the pair of huge lions guarding the gate. Snow blanketed the drive and dusted the trees.

A GIFT OF LOVE

Icicles glittered and dazzled like diamonds and dangled from the bare limbs of the gigantic oaks.

As Dorie drew her pony to a halt, the heavy door swung open and a footman dashed out to take the reins, while another footman assisted the three ladies in descending.

Dorie smiled her thanks and climbed the stairs with a heavy heart. Lord and Lady Thorley always made every guest in their home welcome, but still Dorie always felt a little ill at ease in their world. Being surrounded by liveried servants, the great artwork of old masters, and other priceless artifacts and furniture was enough to set her teeth on edge.

"Dorie," Bella called from the grand staircase. Making her way down leisurely, Bella took Dorie's hands in hers, making a curtsy difficult. "It is so very good to see you." She smiled at Hannah and Rose. "And I see you have brought us two additional helpers."

"Good afternoon, my lady. I hope you are well."

"Now, now, none of that ladyship nonsense. You must all call me Bella." Bella glanced down at her extended stomach. "Very well, thank you, although I do not move rapidly anymore. Now, unwrap and give Barrett your things. I have everything set up in my salon."

Handing her coat and bonnet to the butler, Hannah asked, "Is Ash here?"

Bella studied Hannah's expectant face. "Not presently. He went into the village, but never fear, my dear. He shall return before your departure. I'm sure he is anxious to see all of you." Her gaze stopped on Dorie.

Dorie forced a smile. "I'm not so certain of that myself."

"And you must tell me his secrets," Bella declared with a laugh.

Dorie gulped. "Secrets?"

"He turned such a delightful shade of pink when I asked about his days with you. I assure you I have never seen anything make Ash blush. I admit curiosity is eating at me like a giant bug to hear every detail of his *cooking*."

Dorie laughed. "We shall not expose him." Now, if only Aunt Rose remained lucid enough not to betray her secrets, she would be thankful indeed.

As Bella led them to the salon, Dorie admitted to herself that she also tingled with anticipation over seeing Ash. Of course, he had probably forgotten all about them by now. He was a wealthy marquess with any number of available options for amusement. Could he care about seeing her?

Despite the distance, a few rumors of the *ton* made their way to their small village. If they were to be believed, Ash was quite a rakehell, having broken many hearts.

That was certainly none of her concern, she admonished herself. After all, he was merely a stranger she had assisted when he was injured. There was nothing else to the relationship.

Dorie felt like rolling her eyes and banging her head against the wall. She only wished she could make herself believe that. But in the secret place of her heart that was never revealed, she knew it all to be a lie.

Something about Ash drew her like a moth to a flame, but there was one certain fact. She would

A GIFT OF LOVE

surely get burned if she contemplated anything other than a nodding acquaintance with him.

Mrs. Ainsley was already seated in the salon, drinking tea and chatting. The vicar's wife was a plump woman of middle years with a sweet face surrounded by a halo of graying hair. Bright eyes met Dorie's as she said hello in a subdued voice. Mrs. Ainsley was a somber woman, and Dorie always wondered if it was living with the vicar that made her so pensive.

Mrs. Ainsley's widowed daughter, Miriam, was also there and looked quite well in a yellow silk gown. Dorie shivered. Surely she would freeze in such a thin gown. It had been ages since she had seen Miriam. Since moving away, she visited very little and she never held an affinity for the poor. Dorie wondered what brought her today.

Dorie chastised herself for the uncharitable thought. Perhaps Miriam had changed since losing her husband.

The local squire's wife and daughter were also present. Mrs. Pickworth and Lillian were rigged out in the highest of fashion for such a mundane chore.

Bella introduced the other two ladies as her mother, Lady Marwood, and her sister, Vanora. Both were dressed in the most fashionable style.

Lady Vanora's simple but elegant merino gown contained no frills other than the satin ribbon banding the bottom of the skirt; a paisley shawl was draped around her shoulders. Lady Marwood's elaborate gown was trimmed with numerous ribbons and embroidery. Scalloped shoulder flounces draped over the long sleeves.

Dorie thought of her own woolen gown, faded

and worn. She was as out of place as a sparrow amongst peacocks.

As Dorie rose from her curtsy, she noticed Lady Vanora's eyes grow huge and her mouth hang open as she stared at her. What in the world was the matter with the chit? Dorie wondered if she had grown another head, or was Lady Vanora simply astonished at her lack of style?

As the ladies seated themselves around a table, Bella whispered into Vanora's ear. A flush covered Vanora's face and she turned her gaze to her lap.

"Thank you, ladies, for joining me today," Bella said. "We have a good selection this year with which to fill our baskets. In front of everyone is one of the items. As we pass a basket from person to person, please insert one of the articles. I suggest we begin." Bella turned to one of the maids standing close by. "Ada, please bring me a basket."

The ladies chatted as the baskets made their rounds.

Mrs. Pickworth said, "Dorie, you must be awed that you actually had a marquess in your meager cottage."

"I am just grateful I could be of assistance," Dorie replied.

"It was good of you to do your Christian duty," Mrs. Ainsley muttered.

Miriam passed a basket. "Some would have demanded an offer of marriage after such intimate dealings with a man."

Dorie shrugged. "My sister is too young for marriage and my aunt at an age not to be compromised. As for myself, I have no need of a husband, even if we had not been well chaperoned."

A GIFT OF LOVE 81

Lillian leaned forward. "But he is a wealthy marquess. Any woman would desire marriage to him."

Dorie straightened her shoulders. "I am quite content."

Miriam's gaze raked over her. "One would think you would be most desirous to ensnare a wealthy husband."

Forcing a smile, Dorie said, "I do not wish for a husband I have to ensnare in a trap like a hare. If I never fall in love, I will never marry. 'Tis better than being imprisoned in a loveless marriage."

Lady Marwood sniffed with disdain. "Those are the lower class for you. No regard for the important things in life like wealth and a title."

Changing the subject, Bella said, "Does the vicar have his Christmas sermon prepared, Mrs. Ainsley?"

Dorie smiled a thank-you at Bella. These women reminded her of a pack of dogs on a hunt, and they seemed to scent blood on her.

The last basket finished, the ladies adjourned to sit before the fireplace. Dorie was thankful the conversation had not returned to the subject of herself and Ash.

Mrs. Ainsley sipped her tea and said, "Thank goodness the snow finally stopped. I thought we would be completely deluged."

Dorie walked to the window to stretch her legs. She stared at the formal garden now buried beneath the snow.

A whisper of sound reached her, and she turned to find Lady Vanora shyly approaching. "Miss Knighton, I understand you are the one who rescued Lord Ashborne from his accident."

"Yes, Lady Vanora."

Vanora stared out the window and did not meet Dorie's gaze. "That was very kind of you."

"It was the only charitable thing I could do. I could not leave him to perish in the snow."

"What sort of man is he?"

"I beg your pardon, but I'm not certain of what you want to know."

Lady Vanora glanced behind her, and then whispered, "Mama wants Lord Ashborne to offer for me. I have heard *things*."

Dorie's brow furrowed. Lady Vanora was probably all of eighteen. Had she heard rumors of Ash's rakish ways? "What sort of things?"

Vanora glanced behind her again, as if making sure no one could hear. Her voice grew softer. "That he is a . . ." Vanora chewed her bottom lip.

Dorie laid her hand on Vanora's arm. "A what?"

The words rushed out in a soft breath. "A libertine."

Dorie studied Vanora's huge brown eyes and pale blond hair. Any man would be pleased to have such a beautiful wife. Did Ash consider marrying Lady Vanora? She might be a beauty, but she was such a child. Much too young for Ash. "Lord Ashborne is a very nice man. I have found one cannot believe every rumor one hears."

"So, you do not believe he is a libertine?"

"I think you should give him the benefit of the doubt. There are some who like to tell vicious stories about others. Does your mother believe his lordship will come up to scratch?"

I'm only idly curious, Dorie told herself. *Her answer is inconsequential.*

Vanora's cheeks flushed pink. "He doesn't show

me any marked attention. I-I think I would be happier with a less imposing man, but Mama says I must marry well so we can live affluently. And Mama says that takes a wealthy man."

"Bella married well. Is one daughter not enough?"

Vanora shook her head. "Thor is generous, but does not allow Mama to impose too much."

Lady Marwood would probably have a fit of apoplexy if she knew her younger daughter was saying such things. Dorie said, "I'm not so sure Lord Ashborne would allow much imposition by his mother-in-law."

"What makes you say such a thing?"

Dorie shrugged. "Intuition, I suppose. Nothing specific."

"Then it would be disastrous if Mama forced me to marry him. I shall have to inform her." Vanora twirled around, her gaze searching for her mother.

Dorie laid a hand on her arm. "Lady Vanora, now is not a good time. I would suggest you inform her later, when you are alone."

For a moment Vanora looked crestfallen, and then sighed. "You are correct, of course. Thank you for speaking with me, Dorie. May I call you Dorie?"

"Of course."

"Then you must call me Vanora. We shall be great friends."

Vanora floated over and seated herself on the settee beside her mother. Laughter and conversation floated from the group. A wave of loneliness washed over Dorie. She seemed to always be on the outside looking in.

The drawing room door opened and Ash and Lord Thorley strolled in. Dorie's breath stilled in her throat. Ash looked so handsome in his brown coat with the red of the cold still staining his cheeks. Both men halted where the ladies sat, bowed, and spoke.

Every female pair of eyes gazed upon Ash. Then it hit Dorie why the women were here in their best gowns. Everyone considered Ash a most eligible bachelor for the catching. He was wealthy and titled and unencumbered with a wife.

Dorie turned back to look out the window, though her gaze did not really see anything. She was too aware of his presence to be comfortable. Too aware of every lady's wish to bring him up to scratch. She probably should join the group, but she could not force herself to participate in their gaiety.

Heat burned through her back and the hairs of her neck stood on end. No sound reached her ears until he spoke. "Good afternoon, Dorie. You look quite lovely."

A flush of pleasure heated her cheeks and she smoothed the skirt of her blue woolen gown. The deep voice washed over her like a warm breeze in an icy cave. Her pulse hammered an erratic beat.

Taking a deep breath, Dorie turned, smiled, and sank into a curtsy. "Good afternoon, my lord."

Ash clasped her hand and drew her up. "No need for such formalities. We are very good friends, are we not?"

His heat burned her hand even through her glove. Dorie tried to withdraw her hand, but he held it firmly, like a prize he planned to keep. "No, my lord. Three days does not make us close friends." Dorie wondered if the twinkle in his eyes was amusement.

"Now, Dorie, no need to be contrary. After all . . ."

A deep baritone interrupted his words. "I say, Ash, what are you and Miss Knighton speaking of so quietly?"

Ash gave a smile that did not reach his eyes and said, "Nothing of import, Thor." He laid Dorie's hand on his arm. "It seems our little tête-á-tête has been interrupted and we must rejoin the group."

Dorie smiled brightly.

Then Ash added mischievously, "For the moment."

As Dorie seated herself in a medallion chair, Hannah said, "Is it not good to see Ash again, Dorie?"

"Yes."

Thor leaned back on the settee, his arm resting on Bella's shoulders. "Ash has been quite unkind to us. He refuses to give us the details of his cooking abilities."

Rose's hand covered her mouth and she giggled.

Thor's gaze turned to Rose. "I believe Mrs. Dorrington knows all."

A flush covered Rose's cheeks and she dropped her hand to her lap. Shrugging, she said," "Yes, my lord, but I do not plan to reveal our secrets."

Thor jumped on her comment like a cantankerous cat on a dog. "*Our?* So, you were involved?"

Rose merely smiled demurely and said nothing.

Thor sighed heavily and looked at Hannah. "I suppose the whole family is in on this conundrum."

Hannah nodded.

"Well, Ash, it looks as if you have charmed the ladies to your side."

Lady Marwood said, "I certainly do not see why

you are so insistent on this folderol. To think of Lord Ashborne in a kitchen. Terrible!" She glared at Dorie, accusation on her face.

Ash smiled. "Thor is always in pursuit of something to devil me about."

Lady Marwood shook her head and tsked. "So childish."

Thor's eyebrows rose, but he said nothing over his mother-in-law's comment.

Miriam batted her eyelashes. "Were you in the shooting party, Lord Ashborne?"

"No, I had business in the village."

Miriam cooed, "Too bad, my lord. I am certain you would have killed many birds."

The butler entered and somberly intoned, "Mr. Thomas Langford and Mrs. Charles Peters."

Standing up, Ash shook the man's hand and squeezed his shoulder with his free hand. "Good to see you, Thomas."

"Afternoon, cous." Bowing, he added, "Lord and Lady Thorley." He turned to Mrs. Peters. "My cousin, Sarah."

Ash bowed over her hand. "So pleased to see you again, Mrs. Peters. I hope Thomas has not kept you out overly long in the cold."

Then, Ash introduced the remaining ladies. Dorie noted that Thomas Langford bore a slight resemblance to Ash around the eyes, but there it ended. Rather than raven black, Mr. Langford's hair was more of a dark brown. He was tall and thin. But his clothes were of the finest quality.

Mrs. Peters was a beautiful woman. Her stylish gown strained against her buxom curves. Dark brown eyes swept the ladies and instantly dismissed them. Apparently, she found no rivals in their group.

After polite nothings, Thomas settled into a chair and said, "The weather is frightful. Couldn't stay out riding long."

Rose shook her head. "You must be careful in this weather. An accident may befall you like it did Ash."

Thomas grinned. "Ash has the luck of the angels."

Hannah gasped and stared at Ash wide-eyed. She half whispered, "I knew he was an angel."

Dorie squeezed her hand and said, "I'm certain we are all pleased Providence smiled upon Lord Ashborne."

Ash's hooded gaze met Dorie's. "I am extremely grateful that my demise was postponed and no wild animals burrowed into my clothes."

Heat flooded Dorie's face and her gaze dropped to her lap. It was awful of him to tease her in front of people. She could feel everyone scrutinizing them. Every pair of eyes swiveled from her to Ash and back again.

To change the subject, Dorie said, "It is fortunate that the snow stopped. Perhaps the frigid temperature will rise." Dorie forced a smile and looked up. She could only hope her comment did not sound too inane.

"One can always hope for a thaw," Bella said cheerily.

"I hope not until after Christmas," Hannah piped.

"Before the conversation turned, I meant to ask Miss Hannah a question." Thomas stared at the girl. "Do you propose that Ash is actually an angel?"

Miriam tittered behind her hand.

Mrs. Peters's throaty laughter bounded through the room. "How delightful! Ash an angel. I would have thought him more a minion of the devil." Her eyes devoured Ash like a cat a bowl of cream.

Hannah beamed with no trace of embarrassment or hint that she understood Mrs. Peters's words. "Yes. It was an answer to my request."

"Our Hannah was born on Christmas Day," Bella explained. "She is special."

"I see," Thomas said, incredulousness glinting in is eyes.

He was merely being polite. Did he try to spare Hannah's feelings? Or did he not wish to insult his hostess? Dorie was not quite sure.

"Your cousin seems unconvinced you are an angel," Rose commented.

Ash waved his hand. "Sarah is not my cousin. She is related to Thomas on the other side of the family."

Standing, Dorie said, "We really must depart before it gets too late." Rose and Hannah joined her. They made polite good-byes and withdrew, turning down Bella's dinner invitation.

Dining with that group would have been horrendous. She would have enjoyed Thor and Bella's fellowship, and, if she were honest with herself, Ash's. But to watch the ladies snare Ash would have been dismaying. There was nothing as dangerous or embarrassing as women on the hunt for a husband. She was glad to be spared the humiliation.

The sun had started its westerly decline. Dorie shivered in the cold and urged her pony toward home.

* * *

That evening after dinner, Thomas sipped his tea and said, "I have been thinking about the Knightons. Odd family. One of the maids told me that Rose is a lunatic."

Ash opened his mouth to defend them, but Bella's curt voice cut into the silence, "They are not odd and Rose is certainly not a lunatic. You will not find nicer people."

Thomas smiled and inclined his head. "I beg your pardon."

Sarah said, "It is most kind of you to include those less fortunate, Lady Thorley. But surely, one can do it without inviting them into your home to socialize with decent society."

"Mrs. Peters, I invite them into my home because I truly like them. They are more decent than *some* people who purport to be," Bella retorted quickly.

Sarah said, "Yes, but Dorie is such a mousy little creature. One should consider beauty in those they befriend. Not too beautiful, of course. One does not wish for another woman to outshine her. Isn't that so, Ash?"

Ash sipped his tea and replied, "Not at all. Beauty has nothing to do with choosing friends. I much prefer honest, truthful people."

Sarah stared at Ash a moment, then lowered her gaze. "I had no idea you thought such."

Setting his cup and saucer down, Thomas said, "I believe it is time for me to retire."

Sarah stood. "I believe I shall join you. Good evening." Sarah batted her eyes at Ash and whispered, "until later, my lord," before she took Thomas's arm and left the room.

Sarah was very beautiful and, apparently, more than willing to share her bed with him. But for some reason Ash could not identify, she awoke no answering passion in him.

All during dinner the women had flirted. The unmarried ladies more shyly, the widows more boldly. Each was beautiful in her own way, but he noticed them as he might note an attractive painting. Nice to look at, but inspiring no desire to purchase or take it home.

When he closed his eyes at night, it was sky blue eyes and rich mahogany hair that he envisioned. Feminine curves concealed by faded gowns compelled his body to respond.

Bella turned to Ash. "Is *she* one of your conquests?"

"You malign me, Bella. I never met Sarah until I came here and I certainly have not visited her bedchamber."

"But how long before you do?"

"Never," he muttered.

Bella gaped at him. "Since when do you turn down the lascivious invitations of beautiful widows?"

Ash shrugged and said nothing. He had no answer himself. He dared not attempt explanations to Bella.

Bella sighed and turned to Thor. "I did not want to upset the whole household. Therefore, I waited until Mama and everyone else retired."

Thor smiled indulgently at her. "What is it, love?"

"The Thorley emerald necklace is missing from my chamber."

Nine

Thor stared at her for a moment. "Are you certain your mother or sister did not borrow it?"

"They would never borrow it without asking. Earlier today, Barrett informed me the Botticelli painting is also missing."

Thor exploded. "Who the devil has the temerity to steal the paintings off the damnable wall in my home and the jewels that have belonged to the earls of Thorley for generations?" Vaulting up, he paced to the window and whacked the damask window covering. He turned and strode back to the seating area. Laying his hand on Bella's bare shoulder, Thor squeezed it and replied, "Make sure your jewels are locked up. The servants shall have to be more vigilant in observing everything."

Ash looked at Thor and professed, "Surely you do not believe it is someone in the house."

"I presently have no idea."

"Shall you send for the magistrate?" Bella asked.

"Not yet. Let us find out who the culprit is first. They must have ready access to the house. Everything did not disappear at one time."

A slight movement outside the open door caught

the periphery of Thor's gaze. He froze momentarily.

"Drake?" Bella asked.

He whispered, "Hush," and crept to the door. Looking out, he sighed in exasperation. The hallway was clear, but there had definitely been someone eavesdropping. He frowned and wondered who the devil it was.

Dorie sat by the fire sipping her tea. The day had dawned cloudy and gray. It appeared it might snow again.

Rose sat in the chair beside her, nibbling macaroons given to her by the Thorley cook yesterday, even though it was only three hours since breakfast. Her aunt could eat sugar-laden sweets any time of the day or night.

The logs in the fire popped and Dorie jumped, pulling her thoughts back to more immediate matters. After her tea, she would begin her knitting once more.

Christmas drew closer and this time of the year was the best to sell her woolen goods. She must make enough money to buy a few things as well as make it through the summer, when no one needed scarves and mittens.

It would be nice to make Hannah and the carolers a bowl of wassail, but the cost of the fruit, eggs, ale, and spices would be prohibitive.

Of course, there was Angus's generosity. She had not decided how best to spend those coins.

"I'm going out to play in the snow," Hannah announced from the door.

Her coat looked faded and worn in the morning light. "Put on your mittens and scarf," Dorie instructed.

Hannah sighed and turned back to find the required items.

Attending the festivities at Lord and Lady Thorley's would make Hannah's Christmas special this year. Perhaps Dorie should spend the money on purchasing fabric for new dresses. But would she ever have time to make their dresses before Christmas Day?

Dorie sat in the chair beside Aunt Rose and considered the possibilities. She must do it, for Hannah, she decided. Satisfied, Dorie picked up her knitting.

Hannah trudged back through and out the door. Moments later, the door banged open and Hannah stood there, her cheeks pink from the cold. Wonderment filled her eyes. "Dorie, Aunt Rose, come look!"

Rose looked up from her knitting and asked, "What is it, dear?"

"My angel has visited."

Dorie's knitting needles stilled and she looked up. "Angel has visited?" she asked in a voice that sounded stupid to her own ears.

Dorie stood and Hannah waved her back into her chair. "I shall bring it in. It is too cold for you to come out without your coat."

A moment later Hannah returned with three boxes in her arms. One lid did not sit properly. Apparently, Hannah had opened one.

Hannah fell to her knees between Dorie and the fireplace. She lifted the top on one box. "This package has my name written on it."

Hannah pulled out a dark green coat and slipped it on. Dorie brushed her hand across the fabric. Merino! The finest wool available. Reaching back into the box, Hannah pulled out a pair of ice skates. "May we go skating this afternoon?"

"I . . ."

"Please, Dorie," Hannah begged.

She sighed and gave in. "Very well."

Hannah handed a second box to Rose. "This one is yours."

"Oh, my." Rose brushed her hand across the calico covering the box. "So it is. My name is right on it."

Hannah jumped up and down and demanded, "Open it, Aunt Rose."

Very neatly, Rose untied the ribbon and pushed the top back. She gasped. "Oh, my."

"What is it? What is it?" Hannah demanded.

Rose pulled out a bright red woolen coat. "It is beautiful," she said in a hushed voice, and stared as if it were the first gift she had ever received.

Hannah took the box from her lap and said, "Try it on."

Standing, Rose pushed her arms into the coat. It was a perfect fit, just like Hannah's. Almost as if it had been made for her.

Rose's hand grazed the coat. "So soft," she whispered.

Hannah said, "There is something else in your box."

Rose looked in and pulled out a muff. Rubbing it against her cheek, she murmured, "So soft."

Dorie fell back into her chair and stared at the remaining box. Heat flushed her face. "Are . . . are you certain there is nothing stating who these are from?"

"No, Dorie," Hannah answered, and handed her the third box.

Dorie stared at it. How many years had it been since she had received a gift? Too many to enumerate. When her father was alive, he was too busy to be bothered with buying presents, even for her birthday.

Impatient, Hannah said, "Open it."

"Momentarily. I wish to enjoy the moment."

Pink roses. The box was wrapped in white muslin covered with pink roses and tied with a pink ribbon. It was the most beautiful gift she had ever seen. Tears pricked her eyes.

"Hannah really does have an angel," Rose whispered.

Dorie blinked the tears away and smiled. "It would seem so." With reluctance and a hammering heart, Dorie untied the ribbon and opened the box.

Her breath stilled in her throat as her gaze fell on a deep blue coat. She brushed her hand across the soft merino.

"Try it on," Rose whispered.

Dorie lifted the garment and something gleamed underneath it. She gasped. Ivory knitting needles!

Laying the box on the floor, Dorie stood and slipped the coat on. Perfect. Her hands grazed the length of the coat. "I know these gifts are wonderful, but we really should not accept them."

"To whom do we return 'em?" Hannah asked. "There's no name or address. No clue even as to what store they came from."

"Mr. Cranley might know."

Rose said, "I doubt they came from any shops in our little village."

"Nonetheless, I must ask."

Hannah groaned. "But why? It was my angel."

Dorie inhaled a deep breath. "These gifts are much too expensive."

"If no one in the village knows, we shall have to keep them," Rose noted.

Dorie agreed reluctantly.

"And if we do keep them, may we go skating this afternoon?" Hannah asked.

Dorie nodded.

Hannah hugged Dorie tight, as if she were certain there would be no information gained in the village.

Squinting her eyes, Dorie looked out across the frozen pond. It had not taken Hannah long to slip her new skates on. Hannah wheeled across the ice, a rapturous smile on her round face. Her brown hair streamed behind her like a sail.

Dorie shifted position on the log on which she sat and directed her attention back to fastening her own skates. Neither Mr. Cranley nor anyone else in the village had known anything about the gifts discovered on their doorstep. Of course, she had framed her questions in such a way so as not to disclose the information she sought. Aunt Rose was correct about one thing. Their small village shops did not carry such fine items.

But she had accomplished one thing unbeknownst to Hannah or Aunt Rose. The modiste had two lovely gowns made for a patron that had never been picked up. They would fit Hannah and Aunt

Rose wonderfully. Nothing so lucky for herself, however.

But Mr. Cranley had a bolt of emerald green velvet that would make a lovely dress for Dorie. Guilt consumed her. She should never have spent the money so imprudently, but Hannah would never forget attending the Thorley's Christmas festivity. For she had never forgotten those she had attended with her father.

The house had been full of greenery and laughter and joy. And hundreds upon hundreds of candles had glowed. Many couples had stolen kisses underneath the kissing bough. It was a warm, happy memory. And she would give Hannah one.

A shadow floated over her, blocking the bright sunlight from her eyes. Dorie gazed into black fire. Ash quickly banked the fire in his eyes, replacing it with friendliness. He smiled and inclined his head. "Hello, Dorie."

"Good afternoon, Ash. What are you doing here?" Heat crept into her face at her rudeness.

Ash's black hair was tossed by the wind and the cold had whipped a pink into his cheeks.

He glanced at the pair of skates clasped in his hand. "I thought I might skate. I understand Thor's lake is perfect at this time of year."

Dorie nodded. "Though it has been several years since I last skated."

As Dorie slipped the skate onto her half-boot, Ash discarded his skates and dropped to his knee. "Allow me." He began to tie the skate.

Sunshine gleamed on his silky, black hair. The scent of him filled her head. A giddy sense of abandon welled up from some unknown place deep inside her. Dorie stared at the top of his head and wanted to stop him. Needed to stop him before she executed a foolish act. Before she was lost to all reason and logic.

He was too close. Too discomforting to her well-being. But the words that would halt him and remove him from her immediate boundary would not break forth. They wedged in her throat, thick and choking.

Fingers, strong and gentle, gripped her ankle as he performed the simple task. Dorie gasped at the warm feel of flesh on flesh. No man had ever touched anything other than her hand. It was too intimate, too disconcerting.

"I-I can do that," she managed to mumble.

He smiled, warm and charming. "No need for you to bother. I'm quite capable."

Capable? She swallowed with difficulty. How many women had he charmed? How many lovers lay in his past?

Dorie squeezed her eyes tight and forced the thoughts away. *Think of* . . . What? What thoughts would remove her mind from where it had gone?

The weather! No, that was no good. The cold barely affected her. Her face burned with nervous embarrassment.

"I'm pleased to see you here today," Ash stated.

Dorie tilted her head to the side and contemplated him. The angle of his face showed no duplicity, yet it almost sounded like he had expected her to be here. Impossible! Unless . . .

"Ash, did you by chance leave something on my doorstep to try to repay me for taking you in?"

He looked quite taken aback. "Not at all. What did you discover?"

Dorie bit back a sigh. If he did not leave the gifts, who did? The last thing she needed was for it to become a topic of conversation at Lord and Lady Thorley's house.

Her reluctance must have been noticeable. Ash took one gloved hand between his and said, "You can rely on me not to spread tales."

A smile tugged at the corner of her mouth. "Hannah believes we have been favored by her angel, of course."

"Of course," he replied with a grin. Then, more soberly, "Allow Hannah her fantasies before she grows up and is faced with harsher truths."

Touched, Dorie nodded.

From the lake's edge, Hannah asked, "Did you hear about my Christmas angel's visit to us?" she asked with wonderment in her voice. She shifted her position to look into his face.

"Yes. It was wondrous."

"It was a miracle." Hannah whispered, "I wonder when my remaining wishes will be answered."

"What remaining wishes?" Dorie asked.

Hannah's lips puckered in a pout. "You weren't supposed to hear that." She was aggrieved.

Dorie smiled. "I apologize. You shall have to practice your whispering. Now, what wishes?" Dorie transferred her gaze to Ash. "You seem to know about this."

"I admit Hannah shared it with me, but it is certainly not my place to tell you."

Dorie rolled her eyes. "Hannah?"

Hannah sighed deeply. "I wrote a letter."

"A letter! To whom?"

"My Christmas angel."

"And you asked for . . . *things*?"

Ash broke in, "It was quite an unselfish letter. She asked for nothing for herself."

"Than for whom?"

Hannah said, "I'll be glad when I'm grown up and can have secrets."

Ash chuckled. "Not many people have real secrets. Usually, the truth is found out in the end."

Hannah tilted her head to the side. "If you say so. Are you going to skate with us?"

"As soon as I get my skates on."

Hannah nodded and sailed off.

Ash called, "Be careful you do not skate on thin ice."

He finished tying Dorie's skates and sat on the log beside her to fasten his own. Nonchalantly, he asked, "So, what were your gifts?"

"We all three received new coats." Even though he did not ask, Dorie answered an unspoken question. "I wore my old coat so not to tear the new one."

Ash nodded.

"In addition, I received ivory knitting needles, Hannah skates, and Aunt Rose a muff."

"And you have no idea who left them?"

"No." Dorie studied him. His eyes and face showed no duplicity or deception.

Ash smiled and stood. Holding out his bare hand, he asked, "Are you ready to try your skill on the ice? Hannah seems to be having a grand time."

Dorie guardedly placed her hand in his, and his

fingers closed around it. She stared at their joined hands.

His eyes willed her to look at him. Slowly, her gaze lifted. His smile had disappeared; his face was now dismal and brooding. "I promise not to bite." Lips closed on unspoken words.

What had he started to say before he'd halted? Were they words of ridicule?

"It's not biting I'm worried about," she huffed.

Puckered lips smoothed into a grin. "Then what are you worried about?"

Hannah yelled from the far side of the lake, "The skating is marvelous. You must come."

She debated what to tell him, then decided to follow the easy route. "It is of no import." She quickly stepped onto the ice. Ash was two steps behind her.

Looking behind her, Dorie smothered a giggle. Ash's arms circled like windmills as he tried to balance on two wobbly ankles.

Turning, she skated back to him. "Do you need some assistance?"

"No, no. I've almost mastered it."

Feet flew one way, arms flew the other. *Splunk!* Ash sat on the ice, dazed and chagrined. Red colored the tips of his ears. "I trust you will tell no one of my clumsiness."

"My lips are sealed." She held out her hands. "Let me assist you up."

He looked at her for a moment; then, with an air of reluctance, he put his hands in hers.

"Keep your ankles straight," she instructed. "It must have been a very long time since you have skated."

The tips of his ears turned redder. "Yes, extremely long."

When he reached his feet once again, Ash stilled as if chiseled out of marble and he hardly dared breathe. A deep concentration shadowed his face, as if he willed himself to stay upright. Dorie's hands still rested on his arms.

"Release me," he whispered.

Dorie smiled. "Are you certain?"

He nodded, his head barely moving.

Dorie loosened her hold, keeping her hands inches away from him. But he remained upright. Holding out one hand, she said, "Shall we take a turn around the ice?"

Ash peered at her hand a moment, as if searching his mind, and then laced his fingers with hers. Slowly, they skated forward.

Hannah flew by them, her laughter whipping through the air. "Isn't it wonderful?" she shouted.

"Wonderful," Ash muttered.

Never taking his eyes off his feet, Ash said, "I cannot forget your conversation with Hannah regarding the Christmas celebration at Thor and Bella's. If the cost of new gowns is the only impediment, I would be pleased to assist you."

Heat burned Dorie's face and anger rose in her. Of all the nerve! Then, she quelled the anger. Ash was only being benevolent for Hannah's sake. "That is very . . ." Dorie hesitated, ". . . kind of you, but unnecessary. I have decided to use the money from Angus to purchase us each a gown for the gala."

Ash's eyes left his feet and searched Dorie's face. His fingers squeezed hers. "I am glad. Will you do me the honor of allowing me several dances?"

"Yes," Dorie whispered, unable to form a more intelligent response under his intense gaze.

Joy bubbled in her and a warmth flowed through her. For the first time in a very long time, she was blissfully happy. An energy surged in her that had been absent for so long.

Ash transferred her hand to his other one, wrapped his arm around her waist, and pulled her as close as their skates would allow. Her heart jolted and her pulse pounded.

She was conscious of his gentle grip on the top of her hip. She could not deny the spark of excitement she felt, nor the emotions compelled by this man.

Dorie gloried briefly in the shared moment, even though she knew that seducing women was as natural to him as breathing. He would seduce her as much as he could, and she would be the only one to experience guilt.

As they found the far end of the pond, a figure stepped out from behind an elm tree and raised an arm. Dorie felt a rush of alarm. Beneath the bundle of hat, scarf, and coat it was impossible to determine who the person was.

Ten

"Well, what you are going to do about it?" the harsh voice demanded, piercing Thor's meditation on the snow-covered garden. "Such a servant should be turned out without a reference."

Thor turned and faced his mother-in-law. He loved Bella deeply, but her mother was burdensome. Keeping his voice calm and level, he replied, "We do not know that a servant took your diamond brooch. It could be anyone."

"Everyone here but the servants are ladies and gentlemen. They would never steal."

"Just because a man or woman is born of gentle birth does not put him or her above criminal activity," Thor explained patiently. He had known many *gentlemen* to exhibit unsavory behavior.

A gasp sounded from the door. Lady Marwood turned to the door while Thor directed his gaze to see who interrupted. "I beg your pardon. I did not mean to intrude."

"Ah, Mr. Langford, do come in and back me up," Lady Marwood said.

Thomas entered the room. "How may I be of assistance, my lady?"

"Tell my son-in-law that only the servants would be low enough to steal from a lady."

Thomas blushed. "I'm certain Lord Thorley knows more than I about such matters. After all, I doubt he would hire servants capable of thievery."

"Indeed!" Lady Marwood's voice dripped ice and she turned back to Thor. "I expect you to take care of this matter and my brooch to be returned. Search the servants' quarters," she ordered, "and you will discover my brooch."

"I doubt whoever is stealing things would be stupid enough to hide it in his own room," Thor reasoned. "But I have already instructed Barrett and the housekeeper to begin a thorough search."

"I saw . . ."

Lady Marwood swung toward Thomas. "Yes, Mr. Langford. What did you see?"

He faced Thor. "Perhaps I should not mention it. I should not like to accuse an innocent person."

Thor said, "Please tell me, Thomas. It will go no further." He stared at Lady Marwood. "Will it?"

"*I* shall not spread it about," she huffed.

Thomas continued. "Earlier today I saw Mrs. Dorrington upstairs. She appeared to clasp something in her hand, but I could not say what it was."

Lady Marwood narrowed her eyes at Thor. "There is your thief. Why you allow her the run of this house I shall never understand."

Between gritted teeth, Thor said, "It is not for you to understand my household, madam. I doubt Rose Dorrington is a thief."

"Why, the woman is addled," Lady Marwood retorted. "She will probably murder us in our beds."

"You are perfectly safe from Mrs. Dorrington. She

would not harm a fly. I shall look into the matter. Now, if you will excuse me, I have work to attend to."

Thor sat down at his desk and began reading his papers. Lady Marwood harrumphed and exited in a rustle of silk.

"I apologize, my lord. I did not mean to say anything to cause anxiety."

"Not at all, Thomas. I'm sure there is a reasonable explanation."

"Of course," Thomas answered, and departed.

When he was once again alone, Thor laid his paper down and leaned back into his chair. Even if Rose had stolen, it was not from malice or greed. Sometimes she became a little confused, but he knew she would never harm anyone or knowingly steal. Now if only Bella's mother would believe it.

Lady Marwood sat in the drawing room and fumed. Thor treated her like some sort of nuisance. She was accustomed to everyone doing her bidding and she would not let him dither while Rose Dorrington continued to steal.

The door opened and her lady's maid entered. "You wished to see me, my lady?"

"Yes, Mary. I have a message I wish delivered. Please see that one of the footmen does so." She handed her a piece of vellum.

"Of course, my lady." She curtsied and left the room.

When the culprit was arrested, Lord Thorley would be sorry he had dithered.

A GIFT OF LOVE

***

Ash and Dorie skated to a stop and stepped off the edge of the pond. The cloaked figure's emerald eyes glowed above the scarf. Gloved hands pulled the scarf down and a warm smile was directed at them.

"Good God, Bella, what in the bloody hell are you doing?" Ash demanded.

"Walking. Fresh air is good for mothers-to-be." Her warm laughter filled the air.

"And does Thor know what you are about?"

"Heavens, no," Bella declared. "He would have apoplexy if he did. He has become much too tyrannical these last few months."

"For good cause. What if you fell?" Ash's voice was harsh and critical.

"I am not so clumsy I cannot keep to my feet."

Ash opened his mouth to reply, but Dorie's hand on his arm stilled him.

"Let's not argue." Dorie smiled at Bella and inhaled deeply. "I can understand your desire to walk and breathe the fresh air. The smell of pine and cold is wonderful."

Bella's face took on a look of satisfaction and she glowered at Ash.

"However," Dorie continued, "Ash does have a point, although he conveyed it in a brusque and gruff way. But I assume that is so because he considers you a friend and is worried about you. It is not beyond the possibility that you could trip over a log hidden in the snow or even that your child might decide the time has come to be born. A footman could at least have accompanied you."

Bella frowned at Dorie, and then she sighed. "I suppose you have a valid argument." She squinted at Ash. "You can wipe that satisfied smirk off your face, sir. No one shall advise Drake of this."

Ash grinned at her. "That will not be necessary. Take a look behind you."

Bella squeezed her eyes tight and murmured, "Please, no, tell me he isn't here."

"My dear Bella, that would be a falsehood," Ash informed her.

"Does he look angry?"

"You best put on your prettiest smile and get your compelling story ready. He looks angry enough to wring your sweet little neck."

Dorie hid her grin and watched the mountain of a man descend upon them. His mouth was tight with anger and sparks radiated from his eyes.

Bella smiled her warmest smile and turned to face her husband. "Good afternoon, darling." She kissed him on the cheek and brushed his hair from his forehead. "I see you could not stand being cooped up inside any longer either. It is so kind of you to join me. Give me your arm and accompany me back home. I am ready for the warmth of the fire."

He towered over her and simply stared at her for a moment. Then he held out his arm, though he was still stiff with anger. Bella looped her hand through his arm, pulled him close to her, and began walking.

Lord Thorley's voice drifted back to them. "Do not believe for a moment, madam, that this is the end of it. We shall discuss your foolishness in front of the fire."

Bella patted his hand. "Of course, darling."

A GIFT OF LOVE

Dorie stared after them a moment. "I do not believe I have ever seen Lord Thorley that angry."

"Nor I. But he is always angriest with those he cares about." Ash turned his gaze to Dorie. "I know it is late, but shall we take one more turn before I accompany you home?" He held out his hand in invitation.

Dorie smiled and laid her hand in his. "It would be my pleasure."

Her conscience chided her for allowing this rake to charm her. Nothing good would come of it. A broken heart would be her only gain.

Ignoring the mocking voice inside her, Dorie enjoyed the pleasure of the moment. Tomorrow was time enough to think about reality.

Bella leaned into Drake's arms and sighed happily. Everyone had retired for the evening, leaving them to enjoy the fire of the drawing room alone.

"You should go to bed yourself," Drake said, and kissed Bella on the top of her head.

"In a moment or two." Bella laughed softly. "After all, this settee was where our child was conceived."

"And how could you possibly know that?" he asked.

Bella shrugged her shoulders. "I cannot explain it." She paused, uncertain how to tell Thor her suspicion. "Ash is falling in love with Dorie."

"Are you certain? He may be only attempting to seduce her."

Bella shook her head. "If you had noticed them this afternoon, you would not say that."

"I was too angry to notice anything." Thor

rubbed his hand over her swollen stomach. "You have no idea how petrified I was when I found you had gone out without a footman or anyone with you."

Bella tried to sound contrite, but failed somewhat. "I'm sorry you were worried, but I do get claustrophobic being shut up for days on end."

"I know, darling. I only ask that someone go with you."

Bella sighed dramatically. "Very well."

The door opened and the butler walked in. Before he could open his mouth, Dorie pushed past him. "Miss Knighton, I asked you to wait in the hall," Barrett complained.

Bella sat up. "Do not concern yourself, Barrett."

Dorie faced them as if she faced a firing squad. Her eyes were red and moist, her hands fisted at her sides. "How could you?" she demanded.

Bella looked at Drake, an eyebrow raised in question. Drake shook his head. Bella moved toward her to take her hands and Dorie drew away. Dorie stamped her foot and once again admonished, "How could you?"

"What troubles you, Dorie?" Bella petitioned.

Tears welled in Dorie's eyes. "You know perfectly well. You . . . you . . ." The tears finally broke free and coursed down her cheeks. Dorie bit her lip in an effort not to sob.

Bella did not allow her to draw away again. She wrapped her arms around Dorie and drew her to the settee. Drake placed a snifter of brandy in one hand and his handkerchief in the other.

"Sip this," he ordered.

Dorie did as she was bid and sipped the brandy,

A GIFT OF LOVE 111

coughing as she swallowed it. She took another sip and seemed a little calmer.

Bella sat beside her, one arm draped around her. "Now, my dear, tell us what has happened."

Dorie wiped the tears from her eyes and cheeks, and looked at them with accusation in her eyes. "The magistrate accused Aunt Rose of being a thief."

"That is ridiculous," Bella said. "Has the man gone around the bend?"

"He . . . he did it on Lord Thorley's instructions."

Bella's mouth gaped in shock and she turned to Drake. "I do not believe it."

Drake inclined his head. "Thank you." He sat down beside Dorie and took her hands in his. She tried to draw them away, but he would not allow it.

"Dorie, I have not even talked with the magistrate recently. I certainly did not instruct him to accuse your aunt of stealing the items that have gone missing."

"Missing?" Dorie asked in a small voice.

"A silver teapot, a painting, Bella's emerald necklace, Lady Marwood's diamond brooch," he enumerated.

Dorie stared at him, her eyes wide and afraid. "He . . . he searched the house."

"Fitzsimmon had no call to do such a thing!" Drake exploded.

Dorie twisted the handkerchief and stared at her hands. She whispered, "He found something."

Drake stilled and waited, knowing she would tell him in her own time.

"A b-brooch I have never seen before."

"I'm certain there is a logical explanation," Bella insisted. She stared at Drake, willing him to believe her.

"I am certain you are correct, Bella. Where did he find the brooch?"

"In Aunt Rose's coat pocket. She swears she knows nothing of how it came to be there." Dorie chewed her lip. "I know Aunt Rose is sometimes"—Dorie contemplated her choice of words—"confused, but she would never steal anything."

"Where is Mrs. Dorrington?" Drake asked, not too sure what to believe. After all, it was possible that in her confusion the woman had taken the brooch. But what of the other items?

"Fitzsimmon took her away. He said she had to be confined. He thinks she should be committed to Bedlam." Dorie's voice quivered.

Drake squeezed her hand and stood. "I shall see that your aunt is released. Do you wish to stay with Bella?"

"No. Hannah is home in bed and I do not feel comfortable leaving her alone for any length of time."

"Then I shall take you to your door before I visit Fitzsimmons. I shall return shortly." Drake marched out of the room.

Bella hugged Dorie. "All will be well. We do not believe for a moment that Rose stole."

At least intentionally, Bella added to herself. Drake would straighten the muddle out.

Thor walked out of his bedchamber, fastening his greatcoat. A figure appeared from a darkened recess and stood in front of Thor, feet braced apart for a fight. "I should flatten your nose, you bloody bastard."

Eleven

Thor halted and stared at the angry face. He rolled his shoulders and forced his body to relax. "And what did I do to deserve such an assault?" he asked, forcing a lightness to his voice.

"You accused Rose of stealing," Ash said through gritted teeth.

"If that were true, I would hardly be heading out in this foul weather to take Rose home. How did you know what has transpired?" he asked casually. "Were you perchance eavesdropping?"

The tips of Ash's ears turned red and Thor knew his guess was accurate.

"I heard a commotion and Dorie's voice. I came down to see why she was here in the middle of the night. Something could have been wrong with Hannah."

"Since when is Dorie your concern?" Thor asked, eyebrows raised in question.

For a moment, he simply stared at Thor, apparently unable to find the answer.

Thor said dryly, "I did not realize the question was so difficult."

"It is not difficult," Ash said. "But someone must look after the Knightons."

Thor grinned. "I doubt Dorie would appreciate that statement. She has been looking after Rose, Hannah, and herself for several years now and has actually done an excellent job of it. So, you do not plan to seduce Dorie?"

"Bloody hell, no. You know I do not seduce innocents and I have the distinct impression that Dorie is an innocent, even at her advanced age."

Thor nodded.

"And she is not really my type."

"I thought your *type* was anything female."

Ash frowned at him. "Damnation, you make me sound like the worst libertine."

"Well, if the shoe fits . . ."

Ash quickly changed the subject. "What are you going to do about Rose? I could tell from your expression that you did not quite believe her innocent."

"First, I am going to deliver both her and Dorie home, and then I suppose I shall set about identifying the thief."

"When did the thefts begin?"

"Are we going to discuss this at length? If so, maybe we could move from the middle of the hall."

Ash grimaced. "I do not want to keep you, but I can be of assistance. Rose would never steal."

"At least not knowingly," Thor added. "The thefts started several days ago."

"Had all your guests arrived?"

"Everyone but you. Would you mind seeing Dorie home?"

Ash stared a moment. "It will be somewhat inconvenient, but I shall be glad to if it will assist you."

Thor struggled to keep his voice level. "That is very generous of you. I appreciate your thoughtfulness in being of assistance."

The tips of Ash's ears turned red and Thor smothered a grin. The man was so much like the boy he had known. Due to his father's chiding, Ash had finally managed to halt embarrassment from showing on his face. Except his ears. There was always a telltale sign of it on his ears.

He watched Ash go to his chamber to gather his coat and gloves. How much truth was in Bella's observation? Was his best friend truly falling in love? Only time would tell.

Thor shook his head to loosen his thoughts and continued down the stairs.

Dorie stared out the coach window, even though she could see nothing in the dark of the night. There was little light from the moon to reflect off the snow. But she was acutely conscious of Ash sitting beside her, the occasional jolt of his thigh brushing hers beneath the lap robe.

Lord Thorley's carriage hit a hole and she was thrown against Ash. His arm caught her around the shoulder to cushion her, but he did not release her. Heat surged through her new merino coat and even through her woolen gown, as hot and wild as a blazing forest fire.

Dorie chewed her lip and tried to think of something intelligent to say into the thick silence, but nothing was forthcoming. It was as if her mind had taken a holiday.

"Rose will be well," Ash assured her in a husky voice.

"Yes. Lord Thorley will bring her home, but the magistrate still believes her guilty. H-he said she belongs in Bedlam. How shall I prove him wrong?"

He squeezed her shoulder. "Do not worry. I shall discover the guilty party."

A flicker of hope flared in Dorie. She turned to face Ash. "You would do that for Rose?"

Ash smiled. "It shall be my pleasure to be of assistance to you."

"Why?"

Ash stared at her, confusion carved across his face. He opened his mouth to speak, and then closed it.

Dorie laid her hand on his and said, "I am sorry. I did not mean to disconcert you with my question."

Clearing his throat, he said, "Not at all. I would offer my assistance to anyone who required it."

The pleasure faded from Dorie. Attempting to keep her voice level and free of disappointment, she said, "Of course," and averted her face.

Ash cupped her chin and turned her face to him. "Did I say something to offend you?"

Dorie shook her head, unable to voice words over the thumping of her heart. She was intently aware of his warm fingers caressing her face as he gazed at her. A shiver rippled through her. They were too still, too aware of each other. Her weak mind grasped that she should end the touch, end what was about to happen, but she was unable.

His head lowered toward her slowly, giving her time to object or turn away, but she did neither.

Warm lips touched hers like a gentle whisper, sweet, full of promise and persuasion.

A large hand spanned her waist and pulled her closer, his lips more urgent, more demanding. A fire, wild and hot, spread through her blood. Her arms circled his neck and her hands fingered his hair. Cool and soft as silk.

His tongue traced the fullness of her lips and she shivered under the assault. "God, you taste sweet. Open your mouth for me," he whispered, his breath hot and soft upon her lips.

Obeying his strange request, Dorie did not understand until his tongue delved in and stroked hers. Ash shuddered and she clutched him tighter, aware of nothing but the man and the dizzying moment.

The coach slowed and turned. He raised his head and she slowly opened her eyes. Eyes dark and hooded, he stared at her. Anger flooded his face and his lips curled in mockery. "I guess I was wrong about you. You are not so innocent after all." He released her and lapsed into silence, turning to the window.

Dorie collapsed against the corner, weak and confused. And cold, so cold without his warmth. Her face burned at his cruel words, humiliation welling up inside her even as her lips still burned from his kisses.

Emotion swirled in her, but she could not sort it out. Joy over the pleasure of the kiss. Shock that she had allowed him such intimacies. An even greater shock that she wanted more. For the first time in her life, she cared not for convention nor proprieties. Sadness that to him she was just another woman to be seduced like so many others before, and that he had found fault with her kisses.

Dorie swallowed hard and held back the tears filling her eyes. *I will not cry. He will never know how much he hurt me,* she swore to herself.

The coach rolled to a stop at her doorway.

Ash studied her face, but the dark revealed little. For some reason, she had seemed disappointed with his answer, but he was not sure why. He was not even sure why he promised to assist her.

Within his arms, Dorie seemed small and vulnerable, like a child in need of protection. But his own body's reaction testified that she was a woman. He must stop thinking of her as he did the day he listened to her bathe, imagining her warm and rounded, water glistening off her curves, desiring no man but himself.

Ash closed his eyes and stifled a groan. If only he could take her here and now in the coach without regard for her innocence or his guilt. To ease himself into her would be sheer bliss.

Instead, he had lashed out and hurt her. For the first time in his life, he was afraid. He, Nathan Langford, Marquess of Ashborne, was afraid of a slip of a woman who barely came to his shoulders.

Dorie was not the type of woman one dallied with. She was meant for marriage and children. His hand clenched at the thought of another man satisfying himself in Dorie's softness, her giving birth to another man's children.

Ash opened his eyes and forced the thoughts and guilt away. It was best if she hated him and steered clear of him. Twelfth Night would see his departure from this place.

The clouds parted, allowing a half moon to shed some light. Tension and hurt lined her face. And, perhaps, there were tears in her eyes. Her shoulders were so small to bear so much. She took care of her sister and aunt. And now her aunt was accused of stealing. And he had added to her woes. He was the worst sort of libertine. He deserved to be taken out and beaten.

And why did he offer to clear Rose of guilt?

For Rose. That was it. She was a sweet old woman and he hated to see her sent to Bedlam.

Of course, Thor could handle the situation without his assistance. But Bella would give birth anytime now, and Thor's attention would be removed from Rose.

The gray stone cottage squatted beneath the bare oaks like a plump tart bursting with apples. It appeared the sort of place an elf or fairy might reside. Halos of light glowed from the windows framed by blue shutters, and pristine snow shrouded the roof. A column of smoke rose from the chimney and dissipated into the night sky.

The coach door opened and Dorie alighted. Ash followed behind her and waited patiently while she unlocked the door.

With her face still to the door, she murmured, "Thank you for seeing me home."

"Perhaps I should wait with you," he suggested.

"That is not necessary," she quickly replied.

Stepping through the entryway, Ash closed the door to shut the cold out. Indecision radiated in her blue eyes as she chewed on her bottom lip. It was plain she wished him to go to perdition and was trying to decide how to say so.

A GIFT OF LOVE 121

He would simply give her no choice. He removed his coat and hat. Dorie opened her mouth to speak, and then closed it on whatever she'd started to say.

The ormolu clock on the mantle chimed twelve o'clock. Midnight, the bewitching hour. An hour had passed and no sign of Aunt Rose had appeared. Dorie laid the velvet fabric down and rolled her head from side to side.

Everyone else seemed to be napping. Snowflake curled into a ball in front of the fire. In the chair next to her, Ash slumped and dozed. At least the silence was no longer uncomfortable.

Dorie stood up and walked to the window. Still no sign of Lord Thorley and Aunt Rose.

A soft, languid voice spoke behind her. "No need to worry. They shall be here soon."

Dorie turned to find Ash's gaze upon her. The urge to fingercomb his tousled black hair crashed through her. Ash pushed himself upright and stood. He raised his hands to the ceiling and stretched, twisting at the waist. The lawn shirt stretched and Dorie was afraid for a moment the shirt would rend beneath his powerful muscles.

He had not taken the time to put on a waistcoat or cravat and he had removed his coat, lending an air of intimacy to the room.

He reminded her of Snowflake stretching when he arose from a nap. Lazy, yet powerful.

Bending down in front of the fireplace, Ash stoked the fire. The crackling flames painted him an orangish glow. He replaced the fire iron and rubbed Snowflake's ear.

"It is late. You do not have to wait with me."

Hands clasped behind him, he stood with his back to the fire. "Waiting is no trouble. I wish to apologize for my earlier behavior. It was not well done of me."

Dorie reclaimed her seat and clutched her hands in her lap to stop from wringing them. "Apology accepted." Changing the subject, Dorie said, "I hope Aunt Rose is unharmed."

Dorie held her breath to see if he would follow her lead and talk of something else. Admitting the truth to herself, she did not wish to examine the incident too closely.

"She will probably be cold and frightened, but I'm certain no one would harm her."

"Dorie?" a small voice squeaked behind her.

Dorie turned. "Hannah! What are you doing out of bed and in your bare feet?"

Hannah's eyes moved from Dorie to Ash. "Ash!" A bright smile widened on her face and she ran to him, jumping into his arms. Dorie held her breath, but Ash caught her around the waist as her arms twined around his neck.

"What are you doing here so late?"

Dorie knew she should chide Hannah for her rudeness, but she did not have the heart. And if she were truthful with herself, she was a wee bit of jealous of Hannah being held so snugly. Ash's arms were warm and exciting.

"I'm providing Dorie companionship while she waits for your aunt to return home."

"Where is Aunt Rose?"

"She will be home anytime," Dorie said.

Setting Hannah on her feet, Ash said, "You best go back to bed. It is late and cold."

"May I have a good night kiss?"

Ash bent down and kissed her cheek. "Good night."

Hannah skipped toward the door, but stopped and turned back. "G'night, Dorie."

"Sweet dreams," Dorie wished, and watched Hannah skip back to her room.

"Hannah really is a most selfless child," Ash said. "You should be very proud."

"I am." Dorie settled back into her chair.

Just then the door rattled and finally opened, the wind sending it banging into the wall.

Twelve

Her pale face haggard with strain, Rose hesitated at the door, looking from Dorie to Ash, and her eyes welled with tears. Dashing to Ash, Rose threw herself into his arms and sobbed. Ash rubbed her back.

Jealousy assailed Dorie. Why had Aunt Rose gone to Ash for comfort rather than her? She had only known Ash a few short days.

Dorie turned to Lord Thorley. "Thank you. Did Fitzsimmons put up much of a fuss?"

"Yes. He is convinced Mrs. Dorrington is the thief. Tomorrow his people will search for the rest of the items."

Dorie turned to find Aunt Rose still clinging to Ash. He smiled at Dorie over Rose's head and said, "Perhaps you should go to bed, Rose, and rest. Life will look better after a good night's sleep."

Rose nodded and stopped to hug Dorie. "Good night, my dear."

"Good night, Aunt Rose."

Rose shuffled out of the room, her shoulders sagging.

"You really don't believe she is innocent, do you, my lord?" Dorie whispered.

An uncomfortable haze clouded Thor's gaze and he sighed heavily. "I am not certain what the facts are. I do not believe she purposely stole the brooch, but she does get a little confused at times. Could she not have picked it up not realizing the reality of what she did?"

"No," Dorie said with conviction. "And Lord Ashborne has offered to prove the truth."

One of Lord Thorley's eyebrows rose in amazement. "Indeed?"

Dorie smiled at him and nodded. "He believes Aunt Rose innocent. Did you discover who reported Aunt Rose to Fitzsimmons?"

"Yes, and I'm most unhappy about it. It was my mother-in-law." His expression did not bode well.

"Why would Lady Marwood report Aunt Rose?"

"Rose was reportedly seen with something clutched in her hand upstairs and Lady Marwood believed it to be her brooch."

"Who reported seeing Rose?" Ash asked, his voice low and suspicious.

"Thomas." Thorley glanced at Ash and stilled. "Surely you do not believe your cousin had anything to do with the thefts."

"Of course not, but I wish to question him about what he saw." He retrieved his coat from the closet. "I suppose I'm ready to depart."

Thor nodded. "I'm so sorry this sad event occurred, Dorie. At least Rose was only confined in Fitzsimmons's house and did not face the horror of prison. Good night." Thor walked out the door.

Ash hesitated at the door. He turned and walked back to Dorie. Raising her hand to his lips, he said,

"I apologize again for my abominable behavior. Do not fret over Rose. We shall discover the truth."

"Good night, my lord."

Ash started to say something, but changed his mind and departed. Dorie stared after him, unsure of the emotions raging within her.

Was he the seasoned rake of gossip? She had certainly thought so in the coach. Yet, he had been most kind to Rose and Hannah. Perhaps the truth lay somewhere in between.

The next day dawned bright and clear, though snow still trapped them in a world of white and cold. Dorie paused to glance out the kitchen window. Snow bearded tree branches and icicles gleamed like diamond earrings.

Rose and Hannah were still snug and warm in bed. Dorie returned her attention to kneading the fresh bread and whistled a jovial ditty. The dough was warm and gooey on her fingers. She inhaled the yeasty aroma, knowing that the fresh bread would be tasty once baked. Dropping the dough into a bowl, she covered it with a cloth to allow it to rise and washed her hands.

A knock sounded at the back door. Throwing a shawl over her shoulders to guard against the bitter cold, she opened the door a fraction and peeped out. In the early morning sunlight stood Ash.

Events rushed through Dorie's mind. Aunt Rose's predicament. Ash's offer to find the real culprit. The kisses that set her on fire and touched her soul.

She shook her head to clear her mind. "Come in."

Ash entered, moving to stand by the fire and face her. His cheeks were shadowed by concern. "I hope I'm not disturbing you too early."

"No. I was just making bread. Would you like a cup of tea?"

"Please." Ash pulled off his gloves and laid them aside.

He said nothing else until she handed him a cup of steaming tea. He sipped it and looked as if he were trying to work up courage to tell her something unpleasant. He did not meet her gaze.

Dorie sat down and said, "Please do not be afraid to tell me. I can deal with the truth."

He sighed and finally looked her in the eye. "I talked with Thomas last night."

Her stomach clenched in dread. "Yes?"

"He insists he saw Rose upstairs at Thor's with something clasped in her hand."

"Did he see what it was?"

"No, but Lady Marwood is convinced it was her diamond brooch. She last saw it in her jewelry box."

"Why, if she did not see Aunt Rose with the brooch?"

"I suppose she refuses to believe it is someone in the house. Do you know her lady's maid?"

"I do not know Mary well, but I have met her." She looked at him in confusion.

"I-I received a sense of Lady Marwood not being completely honest about something. I thought perhaps her maid might deal honestly with you."

"Why me?"

"For one, you are another woman."

"So are Bella and Vanora."

"Yes, but . . ." He hesitated.

"What?"

"I do not wish to offend you."

"Please just say it. I will attempt not to be offended."

"Bella and Vanora are quite above her social strata."

Dorie's cheeks burned hot and bitter. "Of course, I'm more on the level with a maid."

Ash sighed. Setting his teacup down, he dropped to his knees and took Dorie's hands in his. So large they swallowed hers. And warm. Staring at their clasped hands, Dorie swallowed with difficulty. She had never dreamed bare hands could be so tantalizing.

"Look at me." His tone almost pleaded.

Meeting his gaze, Dorie was stunned at the wretchedness etched on his face.

He said, "Your soul and heart are far better than either Vanora's or Lady Marwood's. But you must not allow words or attitudes to hurt you if we are to find the true culprit."

"I'm sorry. You are correct. I shall talk to Mary, though I am not certain she will reveal anything. Usually lady's maids are very loyal."

"I garnered a sense of something between Lady Marwood and Mary."

"What?"

"I cannot say. It was just an impression from a fleeting expression on Mary's face."

Dorie nodded. "I shall talk to Mary this morning."

Ash squeezed her hands and stood. "I shall call later this afternoon to hear what you learned."

"You'll not be at Thorley Park?"

A GIFT OF LOVE

"I plan to visit the surrounding area and visit those who deal in stolen goods. Someone may have already sold the other stolen pieces."

"It would be a great stroke of luck if you found the buyer. If our thief has sold everything."

"I believe he has. It is common knowledge that the thefts are being investigated. He would not want to be in possession of the items."

"Perhaps I should come with you," Dorie suggested and stood up.

Ash smiled and shook his head. "You have your own investigation to conduct with Mary. Also, see if Rose was actually at Thorley Park on the afternoon the brooch was stolen. If so, she may have seen some useful clue."

Ash leaned down and gently brushed his lips over Dorie's. She stood perfectly still. His thumb stroked her cheek.

His warm breath caressed her as he said, "I shall see you later."

Once he was gone, she collapsed into the chair and buried her burning face in her hands. What in the world was she to do? She needed his assistance to clear Aunt Rose of being labeled a thief.

In actuality Ash was the thief, for he had stolen her heart. If only she could be certain what sort of hands held that delicate organ.

Thirteen

At Thorley Park, Dorie awaited Mary in the housekeeper's sitting room. Mrs. Norton had seemed surprised at Dorie's request to speak with Mary. But she had concealed her surprise and acquiesced, even offering the use of her own parlor.

Finally, Mary walked in. Tall and slender, her hollow-cheeked face was wizened with years of toil. Fine hair, streaked with gray, was pulled back into a severe chignon with tufts sticking out. Anxious gray eyes darted around the room, weary and unsure. Her lips puckered in a grimace.

Dorie smiled, hoping to ease her tension. "Good morning, Mary."

"Mornin', Miss Dorie." She perched on the edge of a wingback chair, ready for flight.

"I appreciate your seeing me. I know you must be busy."

A slight smile broke through Mary's frown. "Not much. Lady Marwood hasn't yet arisen."

Dorie glanced at the clock on the mantle. At nine o'clock it was still early for the leisured, but the servants had probably been up since dawn.

"I hoped you might answer a few questions for me."

"Questions?" Mary was clearly taken aback.

"As you know, they have accused my Aunt Rose of stealing. Lady Marwood seems convinced that Aunt Rose should pay for thefts she did not commit." Dorie sat forward and touched Mary's hand. "I know you do not know Aunt Rose well, but I assure you she would never steal anything, much less Lady Marwood's diamond brooch."

Dorie took a deep breath. It was best to be totally honest. "Sometimes Aunt Rose gets a little confused, but she would never steal."

Mary stared at her hands clasped in her lap. Dorie possessed no idea what her thoughts were, and the other woman made no attempt to share them.

"When did you last see Lady Marwood's brooch?"

Dorie wondered for a moment if Mary would answer. Finally, she looked up and declared, "*I* did not take it."

Dorie's mouth gaped in shock. She had never considered Mary responsible. Regaining her composure, Dorie squeezed Mary's hand. "No one believes such, I assure you."

"Then why all the questions? First Lord Ashborne and now you."

"We only wish to ascertain the truth and clear Aunt Rose of the charge."

"I doubt Lord Thorley will have your aunt taken up and imprisoned."

"No, but others would see her committed to Bedlam. I assure you my aunt is not demented."

Sympathy crossed Mary's face. "That would be a shame. Your aunt is right nice. Early yesterday afternoon was the last time I seen the brooch. I had taken it out of the jewelry box to clean. Her ladyship is most exacting about her jewels."

"And after you cleaned it, what did you do with it?"

Mary shrugged. "I laid it on the dresser. Half an hour later when I returned, it was gone."

"And you saw no one in the hall when you departed and returned?"

Mary shook her head.

"Where was Lady Marwood during this time?"

"In the drawing room with Lady Thorley and Lady Vanora."

A thought crept into Dorie's mind. It was a despicable thought, but possible. She must ask. "Was the brooch insured?"

"Yes."

"Does . . ." Dorie halted. What in the world would Mary think of her next question? She inhaled deeply. "Does Lady Marwood experience any shortage of money?"

Mary stared at Dorie for a moment, then looked at the ticking clock. "Yes. Her own husband was a wastrel and gambled away most of their money before he died in a duel. Lord Thorley gives her money, but it never be enough for her ladyship. And his lordship will not be coerced by her. She thinks to marry Lady Vanora well and have another son-in-law who'll give her funds."

"It was my understanding from Lady Vanora that her mother wished to marry her to Lord Ashborne."

"Aye. He be right wealthy."

Dorie smiled. "Lord Ashborne does not appear

the sort of man to allow a mother-in-law to dictate to him."

Mary returned the smile. "Aye, but Lady Marwood thinks he will give her anything to look the other way."

"I beg your pardon?"

Mary grimaced. "To ignore his lordship's dalliances with other women."

"She doesn't expect him to give up other women if he marries her daughter?"

"Nay. She expects it to be like her own marriage. She looked the other way while Lord Marwood frolicked with all sorts of women. As long as he provided elegant jewels and gowns, he could please himself."

Dorie shook her head. "That is a terrible way to live and to expect the same for her own daughter. I should rather die aged and alone than live such a life."

"Aye, but the Quality be different from me and you, miss. But, perhaps, you're not at your last prayers yet."

"I beg your pardon?"

Mary smiled. "There be rumors of an esteem between you and Lord Ashborne."

Heat burned Dorie's cheeks. She scolded, "You should not listen to rumors, Mary. Most of them are false, just like that one. He is appreciative that I saved his life. That is all."

"Yes, miss."

Though Mary agreed in words, Dorie suspected from the look in her eyes that she did not quite believe it. "Lady Marwood is capable of anything. She has no care for anyone, 'ceptin' herself."

A maid came to the door. " 'xcuse me, Miss Dorie. Her ladyship be wantin' Mary."

"Of course. Thank you, Mary, for speaking with me."

Mary stood and smiled. "You be welcome, miss. I hope you and Lord Ashborne find the culprit who done this."

Dorie smiled and nodded. So did she. So did she.

Dorie hesitated outside the Thorley drawing room. She had planned to visit Bella, but there seemed to be an argument in progress.

Lady Marwood huffed, "Really, Thor, you could be more benevolent."

Thor's hard voice bounced off the walls. "Madam, I give you enough money that ten poor families could live several years. Perhaps you should practice some economies."

"I have my place in society to think of. Trying to marry Vanora off has quite added to my expenses."

"Mama, really!" Bella implored. "You spent little on Vanora's wardrobe, but I have noticed you have several new gowns."

"Do not take that tone with me, missy. I deserve to be taken care of."

"Deserve?" Thor asked in a low, cold tone. "And what have you done to deserve such? The only time you visit us is when you need an influx of cash."

"That is ridiculous."

"No, madam, it is not. I cannot remember once when you have simply visited Bella. Every time you come, you ask for an increase in your funds."

"If you can but be generous with me for a while,

I will not require so much from you once Vanora marries Ash."

"Ash?" Bella blurted. "You want Vanora to marry Ash?"

"Yes. He is titled and quite wealthy. He is a fine husband for Vanora."

"Mama, Vanora is not strong enough to reform Ash. It will take a woman of fortitude and a great love to mend Ash's rakehell ways."

"I do not suggest she reform him. She will have to look the other way as I did."

"How can you wish such a marriage for Vanora?" Thor asked.

"The two of you are ridiculous. That is the way it is done in our world."

"Not always, Mama. Drake and I are testimony to that. I would never wish such a marriage on Vanora."

"Yes, you can be high and mighty about it. You are married to an extremely wealthy man. And if your child is male and an heir, you will please him tremendously," Lady Marwood sneered. "And can probably name your price."

Thor's voice was cold and hard. "I'll have you know, madam, that I am pleased with our child whether it be male or female. And my wife does not give me a child because she wishes a reward. You make her sound like a bloody courtesan."

"Hardly. If that were true, there would be no trade for the courtesans." Lady Marwood sighed heavily. "They do have a function. It kept my husband from my bed so frequently."

"Mama! That is a terrible thing to say. I would kill Drake if he were to stray elsewhere."

Sarcasm dripped from Lady Marwood's words. "Yes, so I have gathered, which proves how ill advised you are. You forgot everything I taught you as a young girl."

"And I suppose you are teaching Vanora the same despicable ideas?"

"She must be prepared for life as *most* of us live it. She must learn to endure the Mrs. Peterses of the world."

Dorie leaned against the wall, her hand covering her mouth in stunned shock at Lady Marwood's words. Ashamed at having listened so long, Dorie crept away.

As she made her way through the garden, a voice stopped her. "Good day, Miss Knighton."

Dorie turned to find Thomas Langford perusing her. Pushing her spectacles up on her nose, Dorie forced a smile and civility. "Good morning, Mr. Langford."

"If you have a moment, I wished to speak with you. There is something we must discuss."

Fourteen

"Whatever could we have to discuss, Mr. Langford?"

"Your aunt. I have not told anyone, for I feared what it would mean to her." He smiled slightly.

Dorie searched his face. His voice was polite, but something unnameable made her shiver.

"You told Lord Thorley you saw Aunt Rose yesterday afternoon with something clutched in her hand. What could be more damning?" Her body stiffened as she waited.

"That someone stole one hundred pounds from my room yesterday."

"No money was found in Aunt Rose's room."

"It would be child's play to hide money."

"Yes, but it also would have been very easy to hide a brooch. Unless someone wanted it found."

"Are you suggesting someone placed the brooch on your aunt?"

"What better way for the real thief to avoid detection? It is quite a brilliant plan."

"Miss Knighton, how would a person do such a thing?"

"Very easily. Especially if Aunt Rose visited Thorley House yesterday."

"And who would do such an abhorrent deed?"

"The real thief. Perhaps the person who reported Aunt Rose to the magistrate."

He laughed. "Egads, you believe Lady Marwood accomplished such a feat."

"I am not certain what to believe, Mr. Langford. I only know that Aunt Rose is innocent."

"Of course." He hesitated a moment. When he resumed speaking, his voice was soft and low. "My cousin will never marry you, you know." His eyes raked her up and down. "He might deign to be your lover. His standards have never been high. I have noticed he turns down no woman, no matter how ugly or socially beneath him. Your liaison with him can only be illegitimate. You will never bring him up to scratch."

Heat flooded Dorie's face. She straightened and looked Langford in the eye. "You forget yourself, sirrah. But put your mind at ease. I have no designs on Lord Ashborne, matrimonial or other."

Before he could say another word, Dorie turned and marched through the garden, her back straight, her head high. Damn the man.

Rose sipped her tea and looked at Dorie. "Yes, I visited Thorley House yesterday afternoon."

"Think, Aunt Rose. Who did you see while you were there?"

Staring into her teacup, Rose said, "I saw Mary come out of Lady Marwood's bedchamber."

"Did she have anything in her hands?"

"No. Then I saw Lady Thorley in the drawing room. She had angry words with her mother."

"What about?"

Rose shrugged. "I do not know. I saw some of the other maids in the kitchen."

"Anyone else around Lady Marwood's chamber?"

"No. I'm not much help, am I? What will they do with me?"

Dorie squeezed Rose's hand. "We will discover the truth. Ash swears he will clear your name."

Rose nodded. "I believe I shall go lie down and rest."

Alone again, Dorie glanced out the window. Dark came early in winter and soon it would be pitch black. Where was Ash? Had some harm come to him while he was searching for the person who bought the stolen items?

Dread rose up in her that the real thief would murder Ash. It was a very real possibility that he would do anything to stop discovery.

A knock sounded at the door and Dorie jumped, her heart in her throat. She swallowed and rose.

Ash stood at the door, his cheeks flushed red with cold. Relief swelled in her. She opened the door wide and said, "Come in and I shall make you some tea."

He removed his coat and gloves and laid them over a chair. Settling at the table, his eyes watched Dorie as she bustled about making tea. An awareness of his nearness assailed Dorie. He did not say a word until she had poured them tea and perched at the table across from him.

Ash wrapped his hands around the cup's warmth. "I found nothing," he said, disappointment thick in his voice. "I was certain I could discover the person who bought the other stolen items."

Frustration filled Dorie, but she had to offer them both hope. "Perhaps he traveled farther. It would behoove him to sell the items as far from here as possible."

"True. I covered many miles, but in one day I could not cover every place."

"Would he have traveled to London?"

"I do not believe so. It would have taken him too long to ride there and back. He would be missed."

"Unless someone from London met him somewhere close."

Ash looked at her with hope. "Possibly, but he would have to have known what he was going to do beforehand."

Dorie stared into her tea for a moment. "Would it not have to be well thought out to avoid detection?"

"Not necessarily."

"We continue to say he, but it could have been a woman."

His eyes narrowed as he looked at her. "Do you have someone specific in mind?"

"I found out from Mary that Lady Marwood is strapped financially and her brooch was insured. Hiding a piece of jewelry would be one way for a lady to raise money."

"Thor gives her a generous allowance."

"Not generous enough for Lady Marwood."

"How do you know that?"

Heat flushed her face. "I am a terrible person," she admitted.

Ash reached across the table, squeezed her hand,

and smiled. "I find that hard to believe. What have you done that is so terrible?"

"Eavesdropped," she confessed. "When I finished interviewing Mary, I went to speak with Bella. She, Bella, and Lord Thorley were arguing about money. I-I listened for a moment."

"And the argument was that Thor did not give her enough money to cover her expenses?"

Dorie nodded, but felt miserable having to confide her transgression to Ash. He would think her a dreadful person. She stared at the table unable to bear seeing the disappointment in his eyes.

"At least until Vanora marries, and then she will depend heavily on her new son-in-law."

"Not necessarily."

"I beg your pardon?"

Dorie sighed. "Lady Marwood's choice is you."

"Me?"

The incredulousness in his voice was almost amusing.

"Bloody hell! So, you *overheard* that bit of information also?"

She nodded, still staring at the tabletop.

"What did Bella and Thor say to that?"

"Bella said you were all wrong for Vanora. That she is not strong enough to reform you."

"And Lady Marwood's reaction?"

"That it did not matter. She expects Vanora to look the other way from your liaisons just as she did in her marriage. Title and wealth are most important."

"I see. What do you think of such a marriage?"

"It would be very cold and empty."

"And if you married, would you look the other way of your husband's amours?"

"No." Dorie laughed, but it sounded hollow even to her own ears. "I am afraid I would probably murder my husband if he made love to another woman."

Heavy silence descended on the kitchen. Finally, Dorie could stand the stillness no longer. She raised her gaze to find Ash's eyes glittering with amusement. His mouth curved into an unconscious smile. His raven black gaze held her spellbound, trapped like a fly in amber.

Ash broke the spell when he spoke. "I shall try again tomorrow."

"Perhaps the thief traveled as far north as Scotland."

"Possibly. Angus might be of assistance. I remembered him when my memory returned. I'd met him once or twice before, which is why he thought I looked familiar. He buys horses from my estate in Dorset. He knows men that will purchase and sell anything."

"I shall travel with you."

"No, you will stay here where it is safe and warm."

"But . . ."

Ash laid his finger on her lips. "No argument, please. Did you ask Rose if she saw anyone?"

He removed his finger from her lips and she repeated what Rose had told her. She reminded herself she had never agreed to not go with him tomorrow.

"What time will you depart tomorrow?"

"Early. Around six o'clock. I should be returning

to Thorley House." He stood and for a moment simply stared at her.

Dorie tingled with awareness as his eyes bore into her. Seizing her by her shoulders, he pulled her to her feet. Before her mind could form thoughts, he pulled her to him and covered her mouth with his.

Fifteen

Ash surprised even himself. He had never meant to kiss her again. The kiss in the coach had been partially routine on his part. He was accustomed to kissing ladies when the chance presented itself. It was why they called him a rake.

But Dorie's kiss was different somehow. His mind searched for the answer, but it was not forthcoming. It was the first time a kiss had ever distracted him. Kissing her had surpassed all his fantasies.

He pushed the annoying thoughts away and reveled in the softness and sweet taste of her lips. He was determined to drive Dorie's stiffness away and feel her soft against him once again. It might just take all his mettle to achieve that.

Just as she relaxed into him, pinpoints of pain exploded in Ash's shoulder and a howl ravaged his ear. He jerked away from Dorie. "What in the bloody hell?" His hands encountered fur.

Dorie scolded, "Snowflake! Bad boy!"

Ash lifted the enraged ball of fur from his shoulder and gently dropped him to the floor.

"Let me see about your shoulder. He may have broken skin."

Ash shook his head and gazed into her passion-filled face. Lord, it was difficult to leave. "I will pick you up at seven o'clock."

"Seven?" she asked in a breathless little voice.

"Bella said you were coming to dinner."

"Oh, yes, but I can drive the pony cart."

"Too cold and unsafe." He kissed her once more on the forehead, grabbed his coat, and paused at the door. "Until tonight."

Dorie looked down at her knitting and muffled a curse. The scarf looked like it had been knitted by a six-year-old. Her mind was definitely in the past. Specifically, that afternoon when Ash had kissed her yet again.

Exotic kisses that gave a woman a whiff of foreign beaches of white sand and blue sparkling ocean. Of wondrous red flowers and scented breezes. The kind of places she only read about and would never see firsthand.

She was not certain she could serenely face him tonight after his good-bye kiss.

An excited voice interrupted her thoughts. "Dorie! Dorie!"

She laid her knitting down and turned to see Hannah standing in the doorway.

"I found a box on the back doorstep." Hannah dropped to the floor in front of the fireplace and peered inside. "Ohhhh!"

Dorie could stand the suspense no longer and joined Hannah on the floor. The aroma of apples, oranges, and spices filled her senses. There were also eggs and a sugar cone. Unwrapping a block, Dorie discovered cocoa.

"We can make a bowl of wassail," Hannah exclaimed. "And hot chocolate. Isn't my angel wonderful?"

"Yes," Dorie agreed. But just who was their angel?

"The day after tomorrow is Christmas Eve. May we gather greenery to decorate the house?"

"Yes. We will go early in the morning."

Hannah hesitated. "Will you have your gown finished in time for Lord and Lady Thorley's Christmas party?"

Dorie nodded. By staying up late every night, she would just about finish it.

Rose walked into the room and gazed at the food in wonderment. "Where did all that come from?"

"From my angel," Hannah declared.

"How wonderful!"

"Aunt Rose, you are not dressed for dinner," Dorie noted.

Rose smoothed the skirt of her faded brown gown. "I am not going."

"But . . ."

Rose held up her hand. "I would feel most uncomfortable due to what happened with the magistrate."

"But Lord and Lady Thorley do not believe you stole the brooch."

"I prefer to stay here with Hannah."

Dorie sighed. "Very well." She stood up and smoothed her gown. It was not the prettiest or most stylish gown ever made, but it was clean and warm.

Never before had she considered her appearance.

Now, she found a small niggling thought that she would like to be pretty for Ash.

A knock sounded at the door. She inhaled deeply and squared her shoulders, ready to meet what came.

"Hannah invited me to hunt Christmas greenery with you."

The statement shocked Dorie out of her reverie. Her mind had been far away in the dark, silent carriage as she tried to distance herself from Ash. Rather than taking the seat across from her, Ash sat beside her. Too close for her peace of mind. He smelled of darkness and danger of the most tempting sort.

"When did she invite you?"

"While you were retrieving your coat. I accepted her invitation."

"I'm sorry she presumes so much on your acquaintance."

"I do not mind. It is nice to be included simply because she likes me."

"She most certainly likes you. I am certain many people do."

Ash sighed heavily. "At times, I do not know if someone actually likes me or my wealth and title."

A sense of sorrow swept over Dorie. It must be terrible to never know why someone befriended you. Never to know a person's motives toward you. But she could not really afford any sympathy for Ash. She was already half in love with the man and it was a hopeless alliance. And Hannah continually forced her into his presence.

Dorie stifled a sigh, knowing that was not the complete truth. No one had coerced her tonight. She had even looked forward to seeing him.

She forced herself to change the conversation's subject. "Do you still travel across the border tomorrow?"

"Yes. I shall depart early."

"I should really accompany you. After all, Rose is my aunt and Angus was very kind."

"No."

The simple word contained not only refusal, but a strength that would never be swayed. Dorie stared into the darkness of the carriage and resolved to accompany him. She must work out a plan that would make it too late to return her home.

The coach slowed and Dorie braced herself. She did not want to sway into Ash as the carriage turned into the Thorley drive.

Light bathed Thorley Park, yellow and full of warmth and cheer. Ivy swirled around the thick white portico columns. Decorated, the house looked festive and even more welcoming.

"Pretty, isn't it?" Ash asked.

"Yes. Do you decorate your home?"

"I suppose the servants do. I have not spent Christmas there in several years."

"Where is your estate?"

"Dorset. But Ashborne House is not quite as large as this."

"I'm sure it is lovely."

"Yes. The view of the ocean is breathtaking. I used to sit on the terrace and watch the sun paint the sky as it set."

"You don't do that any longer?"

"It's rather lonely without anyone to share it with."

The coach drew to a stop. A footman rushed out to open the door and let down the steps. Ash's large warm hand enclosed hers to assist her down.

The black-clad butler held the door. "Good evening, Miss Knighton, my lord."

"Good evening, Barrett," Dorie said.

Barrett accepted their winter outerwear and directed them toward the drawing room.

Bella lumbered up from the settee. Taking Dorie's and Ash's hands, she kissed Dorie's cheek. "I am so glad you could come." She looked behind Dorie. "Did Rose not accompany you?"

"No, she did not feel well. She sends everyone her apologies and felicitations."

Bella towed Dorie and Ash over to the settee. "Sit and Barrett shall pour you an apéritif."

Ash stepped aside. *"You* sit."

Bella waved her hand. "No, no. I shall sit over here by my darling husband."

Lord Thorley stood beside the other settee.

"Good evening, Lord Thorley," Dorie said and, after curtsying, sat down.

Bella dropped onto the settee. Thor sat beside her and wrapped his arm around her shoulders. "It is a pleasure to see you again, Dorie. Please call me Thor."

Dorie nodded. "I hope your mother and sister are well."

Bella's smile faltered for a moment. "Mother had a headache and Vanora is staying with her."

It was a polite lie. Dorie recognized it for what it

was. Apparently, Lady Marwood and Vanora had not wished to associate with Aunt Rose.

Barrett handed Dorie and Ash apéritifs.

"Where is Thomas?" Ash asked, and sipped his drink.

"He and Mrs. Peters reported having other dinner plans," Thor offered. "So, it shall be just the four of us."

Ash's brows rose in surprise, but he said nothing to Thor's revelation.

Bella grimaced and Thor's reaction was quick. "What is wrong?" he demanded.

Bella patted his hand and smiled. "Nothing. Just a small twinge."

"I did not have time to inquire earlier, Ash. How did you enjoy ice-skating?"

"Very enjoyable. Luckily, a good teacher was at hand."

Thor's eyes flickered to Dorie. "Yes, great luck on your part that Dorie was there."

Dorie sipped her apéritif and said, "Hannah enjoyed it immensely."

"Yes, you were having great fun," Bella said. "Next year I shall be able to enjoy skating."

"Were there any soft places on the lake?" Thor asked.

Ash offered, "There appeared to be one slightly off center, but easily avoided."

"I received your note, Dorie. I was pleased to learn that you, Hannah, and Rose will join our Christmas celebration," Bella said.

Dorie smiled. "I am certain we will enjoy it, especially Hannah. She has seen little outside of our small cottage."

Bella rubbed her stomach. "Raising children can be difficult sometimes. At times, I wonder how Vanora and I are so different when raised by the same mother."

Thor picked up Bella's hand and kissed it. "I count myself lucky to have found *you,* my dear."

How would it feel to carry the child of the man you loved? Dorie marveled. It must be truly joyous. And for a man to carry his kisses further and take his pleasure in his wife?

She glanced at Ash and he peered at her, his eyes luminous and unfathomable. Embarrassment heated her face. Did he have any inkling of her thoughts? If she thought for one moment he did, she would run from the room in horror.

Barrett announced dinner. Dorie took Ash's strong arm and followed Bella and Thor. Ash shortened his stride, falling behind their hosts. He murmured for her ears alone, "You should not look at a man so."

Dorie swallowed the lump in her throat. "How is that?"

Ash just smiled. "You know as well as I what your thoughts were. It would only embarrass you further for me to pronounce them aloud."

The blood began to pound in her temples and her breath quickened. He could not know! He was only mocking her, surely.

His next words were little comfort. "I do not mind, of course. Perhaps one day you will discover the truth of your thoughts."

Candlelight radiated from the table and walls, gleaming on the china and crystal. The scent of pine filled the room. Dorie forgot her ill ease for the moment and enjoyed the beauty of the room.

The foursome retired to the drawing room after dinner. The gentlemen partook of brandy while the ladies drank tea.

Ash enjoyed the closeness of Dorie on the settee beside him. Roses again scented her hair or some portion of her anatomy. It would be a wonderful experience to discover just where she wore the fragrance.

"Am I intruding?" a soft voice asked from the door.

The gentlemen rose and Bella said, "Of course not, Vanora. Come sit and I shall pour you a dish of tea."

Vanora settled into a medallion chair and accepted a cup from Bella.

"Good evening, Lady Vanora," Ash said. "I hope Lady Marwood is feeling better. We missed you at dinner."

Her eyes remained on her teacup and a flush crept up her cheeks. "Good evening, my lord. Yes, Mama's headache is much better."

Vanora's hair was swept up in a fashionable style, her brown eyes wide and luminous. She was dressed in a very stylish gown that showed a bit of milky cleavage. The daughter of an earl, Lady Vanora was a most acceptable woman for a wife. The kind gentlemen of his station married and then ignored, retiring to their mistresses for passion.

No matter where he went, there seemed to be ladies to trip over wishing to speak with him.

When he went into the village, when he went riding, even here at Thorley Park. He was accustomed to the attention, for many wished to trap him into marriage either for their daughters or themselves. But for the first time, it was tiresome. He seemed to think only of mahogany hair and eyes as blue as the sky.

Ash swirled his brandy and stared into the amber liquid. For the first time, the rakish life seemed empty to him. Thor and Bella's relationship was passionate and loving. Thor was quite happy at home and would never consider taking a mistress.

Ash bit back a smile. Of course, Bella would kill Thor if he ever contemplated such an affair.

"What has you so amused, Ash?" Thor asked.

Ash pulled his thoughts back to the present. "Nothing. Just contemplating life."

"A very heavy subject for such a lightweight mind."

Ash smiled at Thor and did not reply to his teasing jab. "As the hour grows late, I should take Dorie home." He placed his brandy snifter on the side table.

Dorie sat her teacup down and smiled. "Thank you for a very lovely evening. I truly enjoyed it."

"We were glad to have you," Bella said. "Do you decorate your cottage for Christmas Eve?"

"Yes. I promised Hannah we would collect greenery to decorate the cottage that morning."

"Feel free to make use of my woods, Dorie. We have plenty of ivy, holly, and"—Thor's eyes flicked to Ash—"mistletoe."

"Thank you."

"The mistletoe is high in the trees. I would be glad to loan you a footman as well."

"Thank you, Thor, but Ash will assist us."

"Indeed?" Thor studied Ash. "Still, a footman or two would be helpful."

"Hannah issued the invitation earlier this evening," Ash volunteered. "I could not disappoint her, and the use of a couple of footmen would be appreciated."

"Of course. You have never been one to disappoint the ladies," Thor stated mildly, and brushed a speck off his sleeve.

The tips of Ash's ears turned red, but he said nothing. He stood. "Ready, Dorie?"

Dorie nodded.

Vanora spoke, "Would you like me to accompany you, Dorie?"

"Thank you, but there is no need," Dorie replied.

"But . . ." Vanora finally looked up from her cup. "Your reputation?" she whispered.

Dorie smiled. "Thank you for your concern, Vanora, but at my age one is not quite so concerned with reputation. After all, Ash stayed at my home for three days."

Vanora nodded and turned her gaze back to her cup.

Thomas and Sarah Peters entered, brushing snow from their coats.

"It's wicked cold tonight," Thomas announced.

Sarah smiled at Ash with knowing eyes. "Wicked, indeed." Glimpsing Dorie behind him, her smile faded. "Going out?"

"Accompanying Miss Knighton home," Ash answered, his stomach clenched in dread.

A GIFT OF LOVE

Sarah brushed against him. "When you return, I shall be pleased to warm you."

Ash stepped away. "That is unnecessary, Mrs. Peters."

Ash and Dorie collected their coats and hats. As Ash handed Dorie into the carriage, he said, "Thank you for stopping Vanora from joining us. I would have had to cancel my plans."

Dorie looked back to find him smiling up at her and she shivered. Again, he reminded her of a wolf.

Sixteen

The horses broke into a canter and Dorie whispered into the darkness, "W-what plans?"

"My dear Dorie, we have a long ride ahead of us in the snow and dark. And I am going to answer a question that has plagued me all night." His fingers interlaced with hers.

"What question?" she whispered, and attempted to throttle the dizzy torrent racing through her.

"Whether your lips actually taste as sweet as I remember them."

"What of Mrs. Peters?"

"To the devil with Mrs. Peters. I do not want her." Gathering her into his arms, he held her snugly against his body. There was not a soft place on him.

"You shouldn't," she argued, knowing she could never stop him. Knowing if she was honest with herself she, too, wanted to taste him once more.

His breath was warm and moist against her face. "I know, but I cannot help myself."

Slowly, his lips lowered and covered hers in a gentle kiss as warm and smooth as velvet. She should have been shocked, if not at his seduction, at least at her own fiery response. But the sensation of his lips was too delicious to ignore. Passion was one emotion she believed had passed her by, and now she was experiencing desire as strong as hunger.

Ash raised his head, leaving her lips burning for more. She breathed heavily, observing his every move as if from a distance. He placed his fingers in his mouth and tugged his glove off. The glove dropped to the floor unheeded.

Reclaiming her lips with his, he moved his bare hand to unfasten her coat, coming to rest on her ribs just beneath her breast. Dorie froze, unsure and frightened like the deer who faces the hunter's gun.

He whispered, "I will not do anything you do not wish. You need only tell me."

Emotions spinning, Dorie relaxed back into the kiss and savored the moment.

Gently, his hand circled the outline of one breast. Dorie stopped breathing as her breasts surged at the intimacy of his touch. The strange feeling shot exhilaration through her veins.

Ash murmured, "Sweet."

The coach slowed and turned. Ash lifted the window covering and cursed at what he saw. "We're almost into the village."

Dorie gasped and pushed herself out of Ash's arms. Frantically, she began to button her coat and muttered under her breath.

She was a first-rate fool to allow him such liberties. He was the worst libertine, but she was unaware of any magic formula to make her resist him. Her scruples were sadly lacking, and she was a sad disappointment to her parents, God rest their souls.

The carriage halted outside her cottage. She clutched her reticule to her chest, threw open the coach door, and leapt down. Her only thought was to escape this man who had such a strong hold over her. His presence was hot upon her back.

Dorie managed to subdue her panic and turn at her door. "Thank you for seeing me home, Lord Ashborne. Good night."

She turned to flee through the door, but a hand on her shoulder halted her.

His deep, dark voice floated to her through the night. "Is there a problem, Dorie?"

Clutching her reticule tighter to her chest, she shook her head.

Ash grasped her shoulders and forced her to turn around. "Please do not take me for a fool. I should not have phrased it as a question, since I am certain something is wrong. I presume it was the interlude in the carriage."

Forcing a smile, Dorie lied, "Fustain. I am merely trying to get out of the cold. I apologize if my manner was abrupt."

Laughter rumbled from his chest. "Any more brusque and you would have bolted before the horses stopped. I know what you are thinking."

Anger flamed her face. "Really? I did not know you were a seer."

"I am no seer, but any virtuous young woman would be ashamed of allowing a man such familiarities. I wish you to know that there is nothing of which to be remorseful."

Dorie raised her chin. "At my age, I have seen much of life, sirrah. I forfeited my virtue long ago."

Dorie was not certain why she made up the falsehood. Perhaps it was because he seemed so sure of his facts. But one thing was certain: It was too late to go back without branding herself a liar. Best to brazen out the situation.

Ash's brows rose in polite inquiry. "And did you threaten his manhood with a fire iron also?"

"I-it was dark and I did not see what happened."

"I apologize for mistaking the situation. I should not have worried over injuring your sensibilities."

Trying to swallow past the lump in her throat, Dorie said, "Quite so." It was fortunate the dim light did not reveal her face too well, for it flamed with embarrassment.

Taking her hand, Ash kissed the inside of her wrist and said, "Until the day after tomorrow."

"Day after tomorrow?" she shrieked.

He slowly nodded. "Hannah invited me to hunt Christmas greenery with you, remember?"

"Oh! Oh, yes, of course."

Damnation! How would she ever endure it?

"Good night." She slammed the door in his face.

The fire crackled and popped, spreading a yellow shadow over the room. Aunt Rose must have recently stoked it. Dorie removed her coat and gloves and dropped into the chair.

She stared into the orange flames and contemplated her situation. How did she always land in these predicaments? That was easy to answer. Her father had always told her she should think before she spoke.

Well, one thing was for certain. He could not very well seduce her in front of Hannah while they collected greenery to decorate the cottage. Of course, she had wanted to travel to Angus's with him.

She came to a decision. Ash would never force himself upon her without her consent. She would travel with him and make certain to keep him at an arm's distance.

She sighed. Perhaps two arms.

Ash glanced out the window as the carriage bowled along. Having gotten an early start this morning, he was anxious to complete his journey and return to Thorley Park.

Tomorrow was Christmas Eve and he had great plans. Dorie would join Thor and his guests for the festivities, and Ash had one thing in mind. To catch Dorie under the kissing bough.

He remembered last night and chuckled. Did she really expect him to believe the prevarication about being experienced? He was not certain why she did it, but of one thing he was absolutely, positively certain, or his name was not Nathan Langford. Pandora Knighton had never been kissed, much less made love to by a man.

Ash frowned and turned his head to the side. Had he heard something? He carefully listened again. *Tap! Tap!* Was someone actually tapping on the partition between himself and the boot?

A soft voice filtered through. "Ash! Can you let me out of the boot?"

He instructed the coachman to pull over.

The door opened and the coachman looked inside with a frown. "Somethin' wrong, me lord?"

Ash sighed and stepped out. "Yes, open the boot."

Confusion knitted his brow. "There ain't nothin' in the boot."

"I disagree. Just open it for me, please."

The coachman shook his head, but complied with

Ash's wishes, probably certain that this particular lord's mind was addled. Ash waited impatiently, his hands fisted at his sides. He would kill her!

Finally, the boot opened to reveal the interior. There, curled up, looking dusty and untidy, was Dorie. Her expression resembled that of a kitten that had been discovered being naughty. The flower on her bonnet was askew. Ash straightened the dipping flower from in front of her eye.

She had the nerve to grin at him. Her grin on top of the coachman's gaping mouth made the situation unbearable. He exploded, "Bloody hell, woman, have you lost your wits?"

Grabbing her roughly by the shoulders, Ash yanked her out, but held onto her shoulders until she found her feet.

Patting his arm, she attempted to soothe his anger, "Now, now! There is no reason to be disconcerted."

When Ash glared at her, she continued, "I am not some lady of the *ton* who has just discovered a fly in her soup."

"Of course not. May we talk about this inside the coach? The weather is rather chilly." Dorie rubbed her arms.

Ash pointed to the carriage. "Get in," he ordered, and instructed the coachman to start up.

Scowling across at her, Ash attempted to intimidate her, but it was pointless. She just continued to smile at him as if he had picked her up at her cottage for a drive. His hands fisted on his knees.

"Now, then, madam, explain yourself." Even to his own ears, his voice was low and threatening, but apparently she was heedless of her danger. Fingers drummed on his knee.

Straightening her coat, she said, "I wished to go with you."

He waited, but nothing else was forthcoming from her sweet little mouth. His gaze dropped to that mouth, and he realized instantly that it was a mistake, for his body clenched in anticipation.

Forcing his gaze back up to hers, Ash noticed the blue of her eyes had deepened. Maybe she was not as sure of herself as she pretended.

"And?" he demanded.

"There is no 'and,'" she huffed.

"So, you ignored my wishes to fulfill your own?"

Dorie shrugged her shoulders. "I suppose one could view the situation in that manner."

"And how do *you* look at the situation?"

Dorie chewed on her bottom lip and gazed at him from beneath lowered lids. "I do not wish to sound ungrateful, but Rose is my aunt and I should have a role in proving her innocence."

"I should turn you over my knee and flail you," he threatened. It was the wrong thing to say, for the vision of her rounded backside under his hand brought him further agonies.

Dorie's smile vanished, wiped away by astonishment, and she flashed him a look of disdain. "There is no reason to be ill mannered."

The situation would have been laughable if his body did not throb and yearn to explore her. He was accustomed to being obeyed, and this slip of a woman ventured forth with no fear.

He squirmed, trying to find a more comfortable position. "No, I should turn around this very moment, travel all the way back, and deposit you at your cottage door."

Dorie relaxed again and smiled. "You would have done that at the very first if you had a mind to."

"Do not be so certain, Dorie. It *is* an option." One he would exercise if he had any intelligence.

Her smile faded. "But you would lose valuable time."

True, but he should carry it out just to exhibit to her *he* was in charge. He bit back a heavy sigh. That was a petty thought and it chagrined him.

Laying her hand on his, Dorie interrupted his thoughts. "I am sorry, Ash. I never meant to annoy you." She looked away and stared at the passing scenery. "I am able to do so little for Rose and Hannah. And this is the most pressing moment in Rose's life. I-I wanted to be a part of saving her."

She took a deep breath and turned back to Ash, her voice quiet and dismal. "In the stories Mama read to me, it was always the man who saved the woman. For once, why cannot a woman do the saving of her loved ones?"

Defeat crashed down upon him like the waves hitting the cliffs and chipping away at the indomitable rock bit by bit. This woman aroused uncertainties within him as well as perplexing emotions.

The women of his world lived their lives in certain stations, never escaping their assigned roles. Was he wrong to deny her?

Everything he believed about women had been learned from his father. He remembered his mother as a fragile woman who bore with stoic dignity his father's vices, but with no joy or happiness.

Ash sighed heavily. "Very well."

Her face lit with anticipation.

"But . . ."

Her face fell.

"You shall do what I say without question. Your life may depend upon it."

Dorie beamed another smile at him. "Agreed. I do not believe I have ever been this far north. When do we cross the border?"

"A while yet. You might as well relax and enjoy the scenery."

As his eyes drank in the lovely woman sitting across from him, Ash knew that was just what he was going to do.

Seventeen

The carriage shuddered and trembled, pulling Dorie from her musings. She grabbed a strap and Ash braced himself against the cushion. She stared at him, her mouth gaping with incredulity. One corner of the carriage collapsed onto the roadway; then it began to slow as the coachman yelled at the horses.

"Bloody hell, a damn wheel has fallen off!" Ash cursed, and stuck his head out the window.

He threw the door open and bounded out. Turning back, he held his hand out and assisted her down. The threesome stared at the lopsided coach, now missing one wheel.

The coachman shook his head and said, "I'll be bringing the wheel back." Henry trotted down the road.

"How far are we from a town or village?" Dorie asked.

"I'm not sure, but we're not far from Angus's home."

Dorie tilted her head to the side. "I meant to ask you how you know where he lives."

"He told me."

"Will we walk?"

He shook his head. "Too cold. Henry can ride one of the horses and bring back assistance."

Dorie shivered as a wave of cold filtered beneath her gown.

Henry brought the rolling wheel to a stop and he and Ash squatted down to study it.

"Lucky we be," Henry said. "The spoke's not broken."

Ash smoothed his hand over the hub and frowned. "Yes, looks like the linchpins worked their way out."

"Do we 'pair her?" Henry asked.

Ash looked around. "I doubt if we can find anything strong enough to hold the wheel on safely. We might not be so lucky next time. You shall ride one of the horses and bring back assistance."

Henry nodded and listened to Ash's instructions.

Ash opened the carriage door and turned to Dorie. "You can wait inside while we unfasten the horses."

Dorie settled onto the seat. The harnesses jingled and jangled as they worked.

Ash climbed into the carriage sitting opposite Dorie.

"Why did you frown when you examined the wheel?"

Ash shot her a look of consternation and hesitated. "There were gouges in the wood, as if someone pried the linchpins up."

"What?"

"Everyone at Thorley Park knew last night I planned to take this coach this morning. Loosen the linchpins enough and they will eventually work their way loose."

Blood drained from her face.

"At least you would not have to suffer my cooking again," he suggested lightly.

"But why?" she whispered, ignoring his jest.

Horror flooded through Dorie. Who would wish such a thing enough to tamper with the carriage? The thought was too horrendous to bear. Then other thoughts crowded into Dorie's mind. If the carriage speed had been faster, they could now be lying lifeless in the ditch.

She took a deep breath and said, "If that is true, possibly your first *accident* was not really an accident."

Ash shrugged. "Unless I remember what happened, we shall never know. Besides, we have a more immediate problem." He took one of her gloved hands between his and massaged it.

Hands large and powerful. Even through their gloves, the warmth seeped through to her own hand. Dorie stared at their clasped hands for a moment.

The quiet settled in her brain, along with a realization. She was totally alone with this man in the midst of nowhere. No human soul existed in proximity to them. But she was not afraid. In fact, a strange disturbance poured through her veins, wild and exciting.

Raising her gaze to his, she searched his eyes. His tone was too gentle, too mild. She was too afraid to contemplate his meaning.

"We do?"

"Yes. We have to keep warm until Henry returns with assistance."

"We could build a bonfire outside," Dorie suggested. Twitching the leather covering back from the window, she added, "I am certain we could find enough firewood or grass."

"Now, that is clever, but I do not have a flint or tinderbox with me." He eyed her reticule, one eyebrow raised in question. "Do you?"

Dorie shook her head.

"So, I have a more practical suggestion."

Dorie knew she was not going to agree with his idea. He was too relaxed, as if calming a high-strung mare.

Swallowing past the lump in her throat, she whispered, "What?"

Ash squeezed her hand, still lingering between his, and shifted to the seat beside her. Breath stilled in her throat. His essence surrounded her. Being in a confined carriage with him was bad enough, but his sitting beside her was sheer torture. Dorie stared at the floor and noted the pools of melted snow mixed with dirt.

His arm circled her shoulders. "It would be best if we share our body heat to stay warm. It could be several hours before Henry returns. I would never suggest such a thing if it were not absolutely necessary."

Was he trying to seduce her? Perhaps his rectitude had been quelled when she had told him she was experienced.

Heat burned Dorie's face at the remembrance of past kisses. Her gaze swung to his, but his eyes conveyed nothing but honesty and truth.

"I-I suppose you are correct," Dorie muttered, not really certain of the soundness of the idea, but unable to offer an alternative.

Time stood still as button by button Ash unfastened his greatcoat. He swung Dorie into his lap and secured the woolen garment around her, bands of steel encircling her.

The solidness of the man was too real, and Dorie sat stiffly, afraid to soften against him.

"Relax and lean into me," he whispered, his breath hot against her ear.

Dorie shivered and pushed her spectacles up. Taking a deep breath, she allowed her back to rest against his chest, the crown of her bonnet grazing his jaw. Untying the bow, Ash tossed her bonnet into the other seat. He pulled her back, his chin resting on top of her head.

The quiet of the winter day lay heavy like a rock. The sound of their breathing rose and fell together like a melody.

"I suppose Hannah is excited about the Christmas party."

"Yes," Dorie replied, grateful for him breaking the magical spell he had cast over her. "I'm not sure if she is more excited about seeing you tomorrow when we gather greenery or attending Thor and Bella's festivities."

"Any sightings of her Christmas angel?"

"No, but someone did leave fruit and wassail ingredients on our doorstep. Oranges are not a common item in winter."

Dorie waited for him to say something, but nothing was forthcoming.

"Thor has an orangery," she suggested.

His hands rubbed her arms. "You think Hannah's angel is Thor or Bella?"

Ash generated a surfeit of heat to make her toasty warm all over, even through her coat. Warmer than any bonfire. Dorie nestled further into the heat of his body. Ignoring his groan, she said, "I do not really know. Mysterious events do not usually happen to me. I have lived a very placid life. Who do you think tampered with the carriage wheel?"

He rubbed his chin against her hair and sighed. "Any number of people had the opportunity, but I cannot fathom who would wish me harm."

"A jealous husband or wronged lover is possible."

Ash stilled. "Why do you say that?"

Dorie could have bitten her tongue off. Why did she have to say such a thing? Even if the culprit was such, the matter was nothing to her. Except that she could have been harmed when the coach crashed. Confusion tumulted through her mind as she struggled to think of some inane remark to conceal her emotions.

Dorie endeavored to keep her voice neutral. She must not let him know it mattered. "I may live in the wilds of Yorkshire, but London gossip travels this far north."

"And exactly what have you heard?" His chilly voice rang ominously through the carriage and reverberated through her.

Was he sensitive about the topic? It was a little late to ask herself that question. Once again, her mouth had opened a quagmire as deep and gooey as the Yorkshire bogs.

"You are a rakehell of the first order. Women fall at your feet. No man can compete with you when you set your gaze upon a lady you wish to woo, even if just for one night. You have loved more women than Prinny owns . . ."

"Enough," he barked. "You should not listen to such vile gossip."

"Then it is not true?"

Only silence was her answer. Finally, Ash said, "Like most gossip, much is exaggerated."

"Of course," she agreed, although she doubted his assertion. She was not too naive to note the way Mrs. Peters ogled him or the way Miriam blushed when Ash's attention was on her.

"I sense a lack of true belief in your words."

"I also have eyes."

"Lovely blue eyes." Ash's lips touched her hair. "But what does that mean?"

"Mrs. Peters!"

"Mrs. Peters?"

Dorie sighed heavily. Was he purposely being obtuse? "A man of your experience knows when a woman is . . ." Frantically, her mind groped for the appropriate word.

"Is what?"

"Willing."

Ash whispered, "Mrs. Peters is not the one I wish to be willing."

Dorie shivered. "I-I think we should discuss another subject."

"But why? This one is so interesting. And you did inform me that your virtue was already forfeited, so embarrassment should not be a problem."

Dorie chewed on her bottom lip. Should she confess the lie?

"Is there a problem?" Ash asked, his soft voice caressing her.

"N-no. I . . ." *I am a Bedlamite!* "It was somewhat of a fabrication."

"Indeed?"

Dorie frowned. His voice almost sounded like a grin.

"And the purpose of the *fabrication*?"

Dorie shrugged her shoulders. "I'm not certain."

Ash pulled her to the side and looked into her eyes. His face scowled, but his eyes twinkled. "I always want the truth from you, even if it will make me angry."

Dorie nodded and smiled. Of its own accord, her hand stroked his jaw, already prickly since his morning shave. Surprise flashed over his face, strong and confident.

"You could kiss me again." The brazen words shocked Dorie, for her mind had never formed the intention to say them.

His thumb stroked her cheek. "That would be a dangerous action."

"Why?" she whispered.

"Chaste young ladies should be careful what they request. I might not be able to stop at just a kiss."

Dorie smiled. "You do not frighten me."

"And why not?" he growled. "If you comprehended a fraction about men, you would be shaking in your half-boots."

She was! Could he not feel the quivers surging through her? Eyes as dark as a moonless night searched her face.

"Very well. You shall have what you wish."

Crushing her to him, his mouth swooped down

A GIFT OF LOVE

to cover hers, hard and searching. Shock pulsated through her and she stiffened. This was not the soft, gentle kiss of previous times, but more demanding, almost angry, as if he attempted to prove some point that escaped her. Whether to her or himself she was not certain.

Forcing her lips open, his thrusting tongue plunged in to explore. A whirl of sensation spun through her, leaving her no longer caring if the kiss was gentle or hard. Only caring that the man she loved held her and kissed her, but wanting more.

Her arms encircling his neck, Dorie relaxed and pressed closer, eager and giving, wanting to tantalize him as he did her. She emboldened herself and pushed her tongue into his mouth. The taste of him was wild and wondrous, as exotic to her as a pineapple.

Ash groaned and his hand slid under her gown to rest on her calf. Even through her woolen stockings, the heat of his hand branded her, burning and scalding as long, tapered fingers kneaded her flesh and trailed to her bare thigh. Dorie was startled to feel a rush of moist heat between her legs.

The bulge of his manhood throbbed and hardened against her hip. Only a few days ago she had believed an animal burrowed in the stranger's breeches. With the awareness of the truth that he responded to her, came a thrilling power. A euphoria until this moment unknown. A yearning to see and hold flashed through her.

Dorie scooted her hips, and Ash's tormented groan permeated her ears. Her fingers groped for his breeches fastenings and he hardened further against her touch.

A viselike grip to her wrist stopped her exploration. Ash wrenched his mouth from hers and croaked, "No!"

Dorie blinked with bafflement and struggled through the haze of desire. Annoyance settled over her and she whispered, "Ash?"

He lay his forehead against hers, his eyes closed, and struggled to breathe. "Give me a moment," he panted.

Seeming to recover himself, Ash opened his eyes and kissed her forehead. "My dear Dorie, this is neither the time nor the place for your sweetness. You deserve a bridal bed of the finest silk and lace. Not to mention that Henry could return any moment."

Heat flooded Dorie's face, embarrassed at forgetting herself. For being so brash and reckless.

Determination faded from his face, leaving in its wake a tenderness and gentleness. The dark, glassy eyes softened and one corner of his mouth tugged into a smile.

A large hand cupped her cheek gently and his low, smooth voice soothed, "Do not fret, my love . . ." Ash's eyes narrowed and he tilted his head. A sigh of regret escaped him. "Horses. We best get ready for our rescuers."

Dorie yanked her skirt down and jumped into the other seat, almost flattening her bonnet, but managing to grab it out of the way. As she straightened her coat and tied her bonnet, she glanced at Ash, busy buttoning his own coat, but distraction sparkled in his eyes. Dark eyes that never left her for a moment.

He winked at her and promised, "One day, my love."

A smile trembled over her lips and remorse no

longer squeezed in on her. Happiness filled her, making her as light and airy as a fluffy cloud.

A group of horses and men halted beside their carriage. Dorie looked out and gasped. Fear raced through her. *A band of brigands had set upon them!*

Eighteen

Ash murmured, "*Do not* utter a sound." He slid his hand into the carriage pouch and extracted a pistol. Then the gun and hand disappeared into his coat pocket.

Dorie bit her bottom lip and quelled the urge to argue. She counted. There were six of them. The giant strangers dismounted and peered inside the carriage.

Another carriage pulled up and one of the giants lumbered over to open the door. A fair-headed woman descended, bulky with expectant motherhood. Brown eyes twinkled as she took in the scene.

"Good afternoon. I am Iona McLaren, wife of Angus. My husband's kinsmen have come to assist with your wheel and I to convey Miss Knighton to my home where she can be warm."

Relief swamped Dorie and Ash's hand relaxed. As he assisted Dorie from the carriage, Ash said, "I beg your pardon, Mrs. McLaren, but your kinsmen had not explained who they were."

"Please call me Iona. Then I must apologize. Scots are not the most communicative of men." Iona laughed. "You must also forgive my lack of a curtsy."

Ash waved his hand in dismissal. "Not at all."

"It is most kind of you and your husband to assist us," Dorie said. "Where is Henry?"

"He was almost frozen from his ride, so he stayed by the fire." Iona smiled and took Dorie's hand. "We shall leave these burly men to mend the carriage and take you home where it is warm."

As Iona tugged Dorie to the carriage, she looked back to Ash. He smiled and nodded. She really wanted to stay with him.

Iona said, "You shall be reunited with Lord Ashborne in no time at all," hustled her into the carriage, and they were on their way before Dorie could breathe.

Dorie accepted the cup of tea from Iona and settled back into the chintz chair. Orange flames crackled in the fireplace, driving out the chill of the great hall. The stones of the square keep were ancient, but endured.

"I hope Angus is not ill," Dorie said.

Iona shook her head. "He was at a kinsman's house, but I'm certain he has already joined Lord Ashborne by now. You were the one who took Angus in from the winter storm?"

Dorie nodded and sipped her tea.

"I am most appreciative of your generosity.

"It seems you have repaid us today," Dorie said. "How long have you been married?"

" 'Bout two years now." Iona patted her stomach. "Angus is most anxious to hold his bairn. Will you stay the night?"

"That is most gracious of you. Lord Ashborne

wished to consult with Angus on a matter, but tomorrow is Christmas Eve. I have a small sister with large plans. I'm afraid Hannah would never forgive me if I was not home for the festivities."

Iona nodded in understanding. "I remember the Christmases in Dorset with my family. They were wonderful."

"Dorset?"

"Aye, I'm from Dorset. My parents were most upset at my marrying a Scot, but I took one look at Angus and knew no other man would ever sway my heart as he."

"Lord Ashborne is from Dorset."

"Aye. I was never acquainted with the family, but knew of them, of course. Angus purchases horses from his lordship's estate."

"Did Ash . . . was he . . ."

Iona smiled gently. "What is it you wish to know so badly, but hate to ask?"

Dorie stared at her hands. "It would be ill mannered of me to expect an answer."

Iona laid her hand on top of Dorie's clasped ones. "Never between friends and friends we are."

Dorie raised her gaze and searched Iona's. She saw only genuine goodwill. "It was a foolish question of no import to me."

"Even so, you shall ask it."

"Did Lord Ashborne have a lot of lady friends?"

"Not a foolish question at all. I do not recall hearing of a great number of ladies."

Remembering Iona's earlier remark that Angus swayed her heart, Dorie asked, "What if Angus had not loved you?"

Iona smiled. "Then I would have become as old

and eccentric as my maiden aunt with everyone whispering why I could not snare a husband. You and Lord Ashborne?"

"We are just acquaintances brought together for a short time by circumstances. Twelfth Night shall see an end to our association."

"Fate may have other designs."

"I do not believe in fate. One's life is as it is because of choices made, good or bad. There is no magical influence."

"How very sad in one so young. I wish you could stay longer and meet Angus's aunt, but she is away. One never knows when she will appear at the door."

"I'm sorry I shall not be able to meet her," Dorie said politely, even though she was not certain why Iona wished them to meet.

As if reading her mind, Iona said, "She can foresee the future."

Politeness bade her not to laugh, but her lips twitched. This was as bad as Hannah writing wish letters to angels. "You really believe that?"

Iona smiled knowingly and wagged her finger at Dorie. "I did not believe either at first, but she has proven herself many times."

Dorie leaned forward. "How?"

"Well, before she departed on her trip, she said strangers would visit, but they would not be strangers."

"What?"

Iona explained patiently. "I know of Lord Ashborne from my life in Dorset, but never met him or you. Angus met you and his lordship only days ago. Strangers, but not strangers."

Dorie rolled her eyes and leaned back into the

chair. "I thought you meant real evidence. That statement could have meant any visitors."

"You say that because you do not believe. She need only hold a person's hand to foresee their future. What do you believe in?"

Fingers tensed around her teacup. Dorie gently placed the cup and saucer on the table before she dropped the fragile china. Surprisingly, the question discombobulated her. "God, of course." Dorie hesitated, then continued. "My father reveled in philosophical discussions. He was the most amazing man, especially for a schoolmaster."

"Why?"

Dorie smiled. "He loved Greek mythology. Hence, he named me Pandora. When my sister was born, he wanted to name her Calliope."

At Iona's raised brows, Dorie replied, "She was the Muse of epic poetry. My mother persuaded Papa to name her Hannah." Iona's gentle laughter blended with her own.

"What do you believe about Lord Ashborne?" Iona asked quietly.

Caught off guard by the question, Dorie hesitated, confused and uncertain. Heat flooded her face. "I believe he will prove Aunt Rose is no thief." Dorie inhaled deeply, aware only of a wish to change the conversation.

Rising, Dorie walked to the window and gazed out at the snow-laden roofs. "I hope we have an early spring."

"That would be nice," Iona agreed. "Would you like another cup of tea?"

"No, thank you." Dorie returned to the chair. "The gentlemen have been gone a long time." In

A GIFT OF LOVE

winter dark descended early and the sun would soon begin sinking into the west.

"I am certain they will return soon. Perhaps the carriage wheel was not as easy to mend as they thought."

"I suppose, or they could have been set upon by robbers."

Iona laughed. "Did you see the size of Angus's kinsmen? I doubt a thief would be so foolhardy."

Dorie sighed and nodded.

The door banged open and cold air bellowed into the room. In the midst trooped Ash and Angus. Stamping their boots, they removed their coats and hats and moved to stand in front of the fire.

"Good afternoon, Miss Knighton," Angus said and smiled.

Dorie returned his smile. "Good afternoon, Angus. You are most kind to assist us."

"Ah, it be nothing, lass, after yer kindness."

"After I warm myself, we shall depart," Ash said.

Angus interrupted Dorie's gasp of surprise. "Ye certain ye won't stay the night. We be having plenty of room."

Ash shook his head. "Tomorrow is Christmas Eve."

"Ash? What of our investigation?" Dorie asked.

"That is one reason we were gone so long. Angus took me to meet a few people."

Dorie's hands fisted on her hips. "Without me?"

Ash smiled and bowed. "I apologize, but you were unavailable. It would have taken too long to fetch you."

"But we are doing this together."

Ash's shoulders stiffened and his jaw tensed as if

he braced for a battle. "The only reason we are *together* today is because you stowed away in the boot. I never agreed you were a partner in this venture."

Impaled by Ash's steady gaze and aware of Angus's and Iona's intense interest, she bit back the words rising to her lips, forced a smile, and turned to Iona. "Men can be so ungracious. They rarely value our womanly instincts."

Iona returned her smile. "So true. I cannot recall the number of times Angus has discarded my thoughts only to find I was correct."

Ash and Angus exchanged baffled glances.

Dorie turned her attention back to Ash and in an inordinately sweet voice asked, "Might I know if you found anything useful?"

Ash smiled, not certain how he had escaped an argument. "We found the stolen items, but the cur who acquired them is gone to visit relatives. I shall return in a few days to question him."

"Who is he?"

Angus answered Dorie's question. "He has a thriving business in Edinburgh and London marketing purloined property."

"Why do the authorities not arrest him?" Dorie demanded.

"Never able to prove anything against him. The Quality would rather get their property back quietly and not raise a scandal."

"That is terrible!" Dorie exclaimed. "He should be prosecuted so he cannot frame innocent people like Aunt Rose."

Ash's voice broke the quiet of the room. "He did not steal the items; therefore, he did not frame Rose. He merely purchased them from the thief."

A GIFT OF LOVE

"But who?"

"That is the question it always comes back to. And we shall discover the answer in a few days. We should start our journey home."

Dorie nodded. "Iona, thank you for your hospitality."

"You are most welcome, Dorie. I hope you will visit again."

Dorie smiled. "I would like that. You and Angus must visit me."

Iona patted her extended stomach. "It may be a while before I can visit you, but I shall eventually."

As the carriage pulled out, Dorie looked back to see Angus and Iona standing arm-in-arm in the deepening shadows. She waved and a warm feeling descended upon her. New friends were always worthwhile and she now had two more.

Dorie turned to find Ash's dark eyes studying her. Heat flushed her face under his steady gaze and remembrance of what had transpired between them in this coach. Is that why his eyes burned like bonfires?

Dorie struggled for something to say. "It will be dark before we arrive home." How inane! Why could she not say something clever?

"Yes," he agreed. "Does Rose know where you have been all day?"

"I left a note so she would not worry."

"That was considerate. Though it would have been even more so to have stayed home where you were warm and safe."

"Aunt Rose has enough to worry about presently."

Ash laid his head back on the squab and closed

his eyes. "You shall have to forgive me if I fall asleep."

"Not at all. I know you are tired after the long, arduous day." To be truthful, it was a relief not to have him staring at her.

"Yes, very arduous and about to be more so."

Dorie started to ask what the cryptic statement meant, but decided not to. Her instincts told her she really did not want to know.

Ash swirled his snifter of brandy and took a sip. Lounging in his bedchamber, he wore only breeches and a robe. The day had been long and fatiguing, yet sleep eluded him. He glanced at the ormolu clock resting on the mantle. Half past two o'clock.

His thoughts returned to a woman he had met that afternoon. Time had bent and weathered her body, but the old woman's eyes were blue and youthful. She had taken Ash's hand and stared into his eyes. "Ye have met the one," she had crooned.

Ash had stilled himself not to flinch from the old crone. "I beg your pardon?"

"The one who will end yer mulligrubs for all time. You must not lose her, for without her ye lose yer joy. Ye will never be whole."

The old woman had shaken herself, dropped Ash's hand, and walked away. Ash had turned to Angus. "Who was that?"

"Me aunt. She be a seer."

"What did her gibberish mean?"

Angus had shrugged. "That be the trouble with Auntie. At times her words need much study to understand. And she never explains."

Ash had stared after the old woman, certain it was imperative he understand, but not having a clue how to decipher her words.

A knock sounded, breaking into his reverie, and he forced the disturbing occurrence away. Too tired to rise, he called, "Come," wondering who in the devil was paying a visit at this late hour.

The door opened and Thor walked in, garbed in a black velvet robe. "Saw your light under the door. Are you ill?"

"No, just cannot sleep. I borrowed a decanter of your fine brandy. I would offer you some, but I only have one glass." Ash held up his snifter as proof.

Thor settled into the other chair in front of the fire. "I do not care for any. What robs your sleep? The fact that you came so close to finding the thief?"

Ash stared at his snifter and swirled the brandy again. "Partially."

"And would the other part have something to do with the person who accompanied you?"

"Henry does not keep me from sleep."

Thor sighed. "I did not refer to my coachman, but to Dorie."

Ash stilled. "I was not aware it was common knowledge that she did."

"Not *common* knowledge. Bella told me. Well?"

"I do not care to discuss it."

"Are you trying to seduce her?"

"I do not care to discuss it."

Thor stared at him, his voice hard. "And if I insist?"

"Then, we shall have to resort to fisticuffs and I

do not believe Bella would appreciate that spectacle, especially at this hour."

"Yes, she would wring both our necks."

Ash looked at Thor and they burst out laughing. "Who would ever have thought you would go in fear of a woman, especially one so heavy with child she can barely walk," Ash teased.

Thor sighed heavily. "I am merely concerned about Dorie. She has no male family members to protect her from libertines."

Quietly, Ash asked, "And when have you known me to take advantage of chaste young women?"

"Never, but something about your reaction to Dorie is different. Mrs. Peters has made it abundantly clear she would welcome you in her bed, but as far as I can tell, you have not accepted the invitation. She is a very beautiful woman."

Ash shrugged. "I suppose. Before Bella, did they ever all look the same?"

Thor smiled. "*After* Bella, all the other women blended together in a blur. If you wish to talk about it . . ."

"I do not care to discuss it."

Thor sighed heavily. "Very well, but I am always available should you change your mind. Would you mind discussing the thief or your accidents?"

Ash chuckled. "No, but I do not know much else to say until we can talk to the man who bought the stolen items."

"Is it possible the thefts and your accidents are connected?"

Ash frowned. "I do not see a connection, not that I considered a correlation. Do you?"

Thor studied Ash's face. "No, but it seems strange that the odd incidents come at the same time."

"Coincidence?" Ash suggested.

"I have never held much belief in coincidence." Thor stood. "Just bear the possibility in mind. Good night."

Ash nodded and set his snifter down. "Good night."

After the door closed behind Thor, Ash stood, disrobed, blew out the lamp, and slipped into bed. He shivered as the icy sheets grazed his skin and impulsively wished for shared body heat.

Without delay, Dorie entered his mind. She had been all hot passion and willingness in the carriage. Ready to give herself to *him* after years of reserve. The sweetness of the union would have been sheer heaven.

Ash closed his eyes and groaned. Such thoughts were not helping him to relax into sleep. Best he think about another matter.

Like who had tampered with the carriage wheel linchpins. But he came up with no immediate answer.

When sleep finally claimed him, he dreamed of Dorie . . . and endless days of passion.

Christmas Eve dawned bright and clear, though snow still bundled the day in a brisk chill. Sunshine glittered on the icy woods and snow crunched underneath their boots. The fresh morning air nibbled at Dorie's nose and cheeks.

A few feet ahead, Hannah skipped, full of joy and impatience, oblivious to Dorie's anxiety in Ash's presence. A few feet behind them, two footmen clad in the Thorley black-and-gold livery followed with a barrow to transport the greenery to her cottage.

Dark shadows circled Ash's eyes, his face pale and drawn. "Are you ill?" Dorie asked softly.

"No. I did not sleep well last night."

"I am sorry. Our trip was tiring."

"More than you know."

Hannah stopped and pointed. "A holly bush." Turning, she darted back to Ash and Dorie and tugged on Ash's arm. "Come."

"Hannah, the shrub is not going to run away. Please do not tug on Lord Ashborne in such a ragamuffin manner."

"I do not mind," Ash said graciously.

"It's not every day I get to spend time with my angel," Hannah huffed.

Dorie sighed. "My dear, his lordship is *not* an angel." Although she was beginning to believe he was a dark angel, for he did evoke some sort of sorcery over her. That was a fact she knew firsthand, but she could not explain it to Hannah.

Dorie tapped her lip with her gloved finger and studied the shrub, mentally selecting the prettiest branches. She began to snip. Collecting the cut branches, Hannah and Ash piled them onto the wheeled barrow.

"Are we going to Lord and Lady Thorley's tonight for the lighting of the kissing bough?" Hannah asked.

"Yes," Dorie answered negligently, as if she had not given the matter a lot of thought. The truth was she had thought about it too much last night. After all, it was common for gentlemen to catch ladies under the bough to steal a kiss. And if Ash kissed her, would everyone know it was not the first time? Ash's kisses confused her and made her go weak in the knees.

Ash said, "If I remember correctly, there are some box shrubs on the hillside ahead," and Hannah scampered off to investigate.

Dorie laughed. "She will be exhausted before we finish."

"At least she will sleep well tonight."

"Ash, does everyone at Thorley Park know you found the stolen articles?"

"No, just Thor and Bella. The thief must not know we found his buyer."

"Then everyone still believes Aunt Rose responsible."

"Those who did so before, yes, but not everyone believed the tale."

Dorie sighed heavily. "I imagine our welcome will be lukewarm tonight."

"From some, perhaps." Ash grasped Dorie's hand and squeezed it. "But not from all. You must not allow anyone's aloofness to distress you. Everyone will owe Rose an apology when the affair is over."

Hannah rushed up, her face red, and panted, "T-there's some i-ivy in the c-copse of trees up a-ahead."

Dorie took her hand. "Hannah, you must slow down or you shall make yourself ill rushing about."

Ash took Hannah's other hand. "Walk with us a moment."

Hannah nodded. "It is all so exciting. Tonight we go to dinner at Thorley Park and see the lighting of the Christmas bough and yule log. Then, tomorrow after the church service, we return for Christmas dinner. And tomorrow is my birthday! I'll be a whole ten years old. Dorie, will we have our own yule log?"

"Yes. We'll cut one after we have collected all the greenery. We still need box, ivy, and mistletoe."

Hannah giggled. "Ash, will you kiss Dorie under the kissing bough tonight?"

"Hannah!" Dorie scolded. "You should not ask such questions."

Hannah did not look the least reprimanded. She grinned and looked at Ash waiting for an answer.

A dull red colored the tips of Ash's ears and he cleared his throat. "Well, uh, I suppose if the opportunity arises."

Hannah jumped up and down. "Then, my last wish of my angel will come true."

"I do not even want to know," Dorie said.

Ash grinned. "Probably for the best."

The joy faded from Hannah's face and she looked at the ground, swinging her foot at a snow-covered stone. "Why don't you want to know?"

"It will probably embarrass me."

Hannah shook her head. "I just asked for a husband for you."

Dorie stopped as if frozen to the ground and stared at Hannah. Her cheeks burned with embarrassment. "A husband?" she squeaked.

Hannah nodded and grinned, obviously pleased with herself. "You take such good care of me and Aunt Rose, but you need someone to take care of you."

"I can take care of myself, thank you."

"You're angry," Hannah noted.

Looking past Hannah, Dorie saw amusement

dancing in Ash's dark eyes. "Dear Hannah, one does not receive anything in this world by wishing for it."

"But we received everything else in my letter."

"Pure happenstance."

"Some people do not believe in coincidences," Ash said, and looked at Dorie. "Do we determine our course in life or is life what is fated?"

"We decide our own life by the decisions we achieve," Dorie said, certain she was right. Fate reserved no place in her life.

Hannah sighed and rolled her eyes in disgust. "Old people! It's very simple. You don't *see* the magic because you don't believe in it."

"Old people!" Ash said, and tweaked her nose. "For your information, young lady, we are not old."

Hannah snorted. "The ivy is just ahead." Pulling her hand free, Hannah skipped forward.

Ash finally pulled his gaze away from Hannah's retreating back and met Dorie's. "Perhaps she is right. If one does not believe in the magical, one certainly will never experience it."

His words surprised Dorie. She was saved from having to reply by the appearance of the ivy-covered trees; she immediately began snipping ivy, pushing the conversation from her mind, for her life was void of magic and she held no desire to think on it.

But the notion would not be exorcised completely. Her thoughts returned to just yesterday when Ash had kissed her and caressed her. He created some sort of sorcery over her that could not be suppressed or controlled. And deep in her heart and soul, she knew she would eagerly lie in his arms again. Regret might come later when Ash was gone, but she would hold a precious memory to warm her in the cold, lonely years ahead.

"Are you going to ivy the whole cottage?" Ash asked, chuckling.

Dorie looked up and her eyes widened at the massive mound of ivy accumulated beside her. Heat staining her cheeks, Dorie said, "Well, I guess that is enough ivy. We best move ahead to the hillside for the box." Turning on her heel, Dorie marched ahead, leaving them to collect the ivy.

Dorie found the box-covered hillside and began to clip the shrubs.

Awareness rippled through Dorie as Ash's deep, sensual voice eddied around her. "What is amiss?"

She answered, "Nothing," and continued shearing box branches without glancing up. *I must not look at him. Then, his sorcery will not work and I will be safe.*

Large hands settled on her shoulders and squeezed. Dorie stopped cutting and leaned back against Ash, strong and solid behind her. "You should not lie to me, Dorie."

"You cannot wish to know my every thought."

"Why not? I would find it interesting."

Dorie laughed. "I doubt that. Some of my thoughts are quite banal."

"Now that I doubt." Ash squeezed her shoulders again and informed her, "We are standing under mistletoe. I am required to kiss you."

"B-but Hannah . . ."

"She and the footmen are still collecting the ivy you cut."

He swung her around, his arm firmly around her waist. Dark eyes gleamed with tenderness and passion. His lips touched hers like a whisper, warm and velvety. Once again, he was the sorcerer weaving his magical incantation.

She clutched at his shoulders, trying to moor herself in the raging storm. Once again, she was lost in the whirlpool of emotion he concocted. Her mind quit functioning, aware only of Ash and the yearning he generated.

Nineteen

He drew away, leaving her burning with fire. Eyes dark and wistful, Ash stroked her cheek with his knuckle. "One day, my love," he vowed.

"Dooorriee . . ." The youthful squeal broke the spell.

"Dooorriee, where are you?"

Dorie stepped back and moistened her dry lips. Mistake. The taste of Ash still lingered on her. Her voice quavered on her answer. "Over here, Hannah." And she turned back to cutting the box, unsure if her agitation would go unnoticed under Hannah's scrutiny.

"Ohhh, look Ash, mistletoe!" Hannah cried.

Ash looked above his head and feigned surprise. "So it is. That means you must kiss me." He stooped down and held out his arms. Hannah walked into them and kissed his cheek.

Giggling, Hannah said, "Now, it's Dorie's turn."

Ash cleared his throat. "I'm afraid your sister's turn will have to wait."

"Why?"

Ash cleared his throat again. "Isn't it enough that I say so?"

A GIFT OF LOVE

"No."

Dorie stifled a giggle and continued clipping. Ash frowned at her. Apparently, he was unaccustomed to a child's unrelenting forthrightness.

"Well, I am afraid that answer will have to do."

Hannah frowned. "Why?"

"Why don't you run ahead and find some laurel?"

Hannah sighed and kicked at a fluff of snow. "Very well."

Ash stared after her retreating back. "Doesn't give an inch, does she?"

"No. I am surprised she let you off so easily and did not demand further explanation." Dorie looked at her pile of box clippings. "I believe that is enough."

"Let one of the footmen collect those. It is time I saw to the mistletoe."

Ash and Dorie walked further into the copse of trees where the mistletoe was bountiful and not too high.

"Would you like me to climb the tree, my lord?" the footman asked.

"No, I shall do it myself," Ash informed him, much to the servant's surprise.

Ash removed his hat, gloves, greatcoat, and coat. He handed each item to Dorie. Then he rolled up his sleeves, revealing powerful arms sprinkled with dark, silky hairs. "You shall freeze," she warned him, peering over the burden of clothes. His only reply was a grin.

Standing under a tree, Ash looked up and raised his arms, judging the distance. He bent his knees and vaulted up, catching a limb in his hands. He pulled himself up and sat upon the limb.

Dorie held her breath while she watched him, praying the limb would not break and he would not fall.

Ash smiled down. "A piece of cake."

"What is he doing?" Hannah softly asked.

"Getting your mistletoe, you urchin. How did you think one collected mistletoe from trees?" Ash teased.

Hannah shrugged. "I never really thought about it. You're awfully high. Aren't you afraid?"

"No." He grabbed the limb above him and stood. One boot slid, but he held fast. Blood drained from his face.

Dorie's heart skipped a beat. "Ash?"

He forced a smile, but it was sickly at best. "No need to worry."

"Be careful. You're not a monkey," Dorie admonished.

"And where have you seen monkeys?" Ash asked.

"That is a ridiculous question at this time," she reprimanded.

"Well, 'tis a better thought than wondering if my head is hard enough to withstand a crack on the ground."

Dorie sighed. "In books. Do you have a knife to cut the mistletoe?"

"Yes. Damnation!" Ash swore.

"What happened?"

"Nothing."

Ash climbed further up the tree and began cutting. Hannah and the footmen gathered the white-berried vegetation as it cascaded down. Dorie never took her eyes off Ash, observing his every move as if to safeguard him.

A GIFT OF LOVE

"Is that enough?" Ash called down.

"Yes," Dorie replied.

Cautiously, and with great attention to the placement of his feet and hands, Ash lowered himself from limb to limb. He placed his hands on the last limb and jumped, allowing his body to swing, and then dropped to the ground.

A streak of red dribbled down his arm, dripping from one finger, blotting the pristine snow. Dorie dropped his clothes and seized his arm. "You're bleeding."

"Just a small scratch," he said, and tugged his arm away.

She grabbed it back. "We must see about it." Dorie stooped and scooped up a handful of snow. She gently washed the blood from his arm. "Do you have a handkerchief?"

"In my coat pocket."

"Hannah, please get it for me," Dorie instructed.

Hannah dug through his coat pocket and handed Dorie the handkerchief. Dorie folded it and placed it over the scrape. "Hold this," she ordered.

When his fingers were against the cloth, Dorie bent and ripped a ruffle from her petticoat. She tied the linen around his arm. She patted it. "That should hold the handkerchief in place."

Ash stared at the furbelow decorating his arm. Finally, he glanced at Dorie and softly said, "Thank you." He rolled his sleeves down.

Dorie held his opened coat out and he slipped his arms in. Then, she did the same with his greatcoat. He placed his hat on his head and tapped it. Turning to Hannah, Ash asked, "Did you find any laurel?"

Hannah nodded. "Not too far ahead."

Ash and Dorie walked on and collected the laurel. Dorie said, "That's everything but the yule log."

"There were some ash trees close to where we entered the woods."

Dorie nodded and glanced around. "Where is Hannah?"

Ash instructed the footmen to meet them at the copse of ash trees. Then he also perused the trees. "Maybe she is back at the copse."

They followed their own footsteps back, the only sound their feet crunching on the snow. Dorie called, "Hannah!" Her voice echoed through the silent woods.

Ash grasped Dorie's arm and held her immobile. "Listen," he whispered.

The voice was so small and quiet she almost missed it. "D-Dorie. A-Ash." The frightened utterance had come from . . . Dorie's mind slowly calculated and her face pivoted up. Dorie gasped and panic shivered through her, cutting off her breathing. Fear, cold and dark, knotted her stomach.

On a limb of a tree stood Hannah. Arms hugged the trunk, her face as pale as the snow, her dress torn, and her cheek pressed into the bark.

"What are you doing up there, urchin?" Ash asked, making his voice light and carefree.

Shocked by his unconcerned attitude, Dorie's eyes flew to his, but his dark eyes glimmered with distress and his brow knitted with consternation.

"You made it look so easy," Hannah whimpered, "and I wanted my own mistletoe so Will would have to kiss me."

Ash turned questioning eyes to Dorie. "Will?"

"A boy in the village." Dorie rolled her eyes. "You are too young to be kissing boys," she chastised.

Dorie's gaze reverted to Hannah and she forced a lightness to her own voice through the pulsing knot of terror. "Ash is an angel, Hannah. Of course, it was effortless for him."

"I-I didn't think of that."

"Shall we leave the ragamuffin there, Dorie?" Ash teased.

Hannah giggled. "You wouldn't do that." Her words were certain and sure.

Once again Ash divested himself of greatcoat, coat, and hat and rolled up his sleeves. He vaulted into the tree and commenced to climb to the limb where Hannah stood fixed.

Her arms wrapped rigidly around Ash's greatcoat, Dorie pressed her cheek into the wool and peered up. It was such a long drop down should Hannah fall.

A memory warmed Dorie for a moment. As a child of ten, she had climbed a tree to rescue her kitten. Fear had frozen her on a weak limb. Papa had climbed the tree to rescue the pair of them— and she had never climbed a tree again.

She tugged herself back from the reminiscence and turned her concentration back to the scenario unfolding fifteen feet off the ground. Ash stood behind Hannah, his hands on her shoulders, talking quietly to her, but the words were not discernible to Dorie. Hannah nodded once, turned and wrapped her arms around Ash's neck, and laid her cheek against the back of his head.

Gingerly, Ash scaled each limb until his feet finally

touched the ground. Dorie sighed in relief. A great burden lifted from her shoulders.

Grabbing Hannah's wrists, Ash carefully lowered her to stand. Jumping up, Hannah hugged Ash.

"Thankyouthankyouthankyou!" she squealed. "You were wonderful. Wasn't he, Dorie?"

"Yes," Dorie quietly agreed. "Wonderful!"

Dark eyes blazed brilliant with heated passion and promises as Ash's fiery gaze raked over her.

Ash turned his attention back to Hannah and tweaked her nose. "No more tree climbing for you, young lady," he gently admonished. "Promise me."

Hannah nodded. Dorie pulled Hannah into her arms and held her tight. "You should never do anything so foolish again."

Hannah squirmed from Dorie's embrace. "I shan't."

Taking Hannah's hand in his, Ash said, "And you'll not be kissing any lads either. Your sister is correct. You are much too young for such foolishness."

"But grown-ups kiss all the time," Hannah countered. "They don't consider it foolishness."

"What adults have you seen kissing?" Dorie demanded.

"Lord Thorley is always kissing Lady Thorley when he thinks no one else is around."

"And how do you know that?" Ash questioned.

Hannah's face flushed pink and she stared at the ground.

"Hannah, you haven't been spying on them, have you?" Dorie asked softly.

"Not exactly." Hannah kicked at a tuft of snow.

"*Exactly* what have you been doing, young lady?"

Twenty

"Well, I see them out walking all the time and he is constantly kissing her." Hannah shrugged her shoulders. "I never stick around to watch them."

Ash coughed. Dorie suspected it covered laughter. "Ladies, shall we head toward your home?"

"But the yule log!" Hannah cried.

"Never fear. We are going to cut a yule log," Ash reassured.

They walked in serene companionship. The grating *kree-arit* and rapid *eck-eck-eck* of a grey partridge erupted in the silence. Snow crunched underneath their steps. As they neared the beginning of the Thorley woods, Ash pointed and said, "There's a nice ash tree that should make a good yule log."

Hannah studied the tree. "Isn't it somewhat small?"

"It must fit our fireplace," Dorie said.

"I suppose," Hannah reluctantly agreed.

Ash motioned to one of the footmen and he handed him an ax. "Move back a little," Ash instructed them, and Dorie pulled Hannah a few feet back.

He swung the ax back and forth. Sweat broke out

on his brow. Finally, the tree toppled, crashing to the ground in a spatter of snow. Ash hewed the limbs off and tied ropes around the trunk.

"Who will decorate the log?" Ash asked.

Hannah jumped up and down. "Me! Me!" Picking up some of the ivy and laurel, Hannah wound it along the log. She tilted her head from side to side, studying her handiwork. "That shall do. Dorie said we may have hot chocolate when we return home," Hannah informed Ash.

Ash grinned. "Wonderful!" He handed a footman one of the ropes, and Hannah rushed over to grasp the rope behind him.

Ash looked at Dorie from beneath hooded lashes. "Seems you are stuck with me."

Pretending not to understand his heated look, Dorie smiled and walked without haste to clasp the rope behind Ash. "All right, ladies and gents, on the count of three put all your might into pulling. One. Two. Three!"

Hannah grunted and Dorie ground her teeth in her struggle. The log slowly began to budge under their energy.

A silken cocoon of euphoria swaddled Dorie. Today, no shadows haunted her heart. Life was more of a joy and she perceived the reason all too clearly. Ash. For twelve more days she could enjoy his companionship. On Twelfth Night he returned to Dorset.

She pondered what would be the least hurtful to herself. To enjoy his remaining time or to see him no more. An answer came instantly. Savor every minute in his company and deal with the heartbreak later. After all, love was a one-time proposition and the present was her chance for a forbidden taste of bliss.

Dorie sniffed the aromatic steam of her hot cocoa. Closing her eyes, she sipped it and allowed the flavor to roll over her tongue. It had been eons since she had partaken of a cup of hot cocoa, and the experience was delectable.

"Good?" Ash asked, amusement deep in his voice.

Dorie grinned and opened her eyes. "Good is too bland a word to describe the sensation. Wonderful. Marvelous."

"Divine," Aunt Rose added.

"I now know I only need chocolate to please you ladies. And what of you, Hannah? Are you enjoying your treat?"

A mustache of cocoa curved over her smile. "Spectacular."

Dorie sat her empty cup down and surveyed her domain. Holly, ivy, and laurel garnished the room, adding a cheeriness. The kissing bough hung from the ceiling, candles glowing against the green foliage, red apples, and white and red berries.

Aunt Rose picked up Dorie's cup and walked across the room. Ash ordered, "Stop right there."

Rose froze, her eyes huge as she watched Ash approach her. He smiled and said, "You are under the kissing bough," and kissed her cheek.

Rose blushed and giggled and scurried to the kitchen.

Ash clasped Dorie's hand between his large, rough ones. Exhilaration shot up her arm and her face burned with fire. "May I pick you up this afternoon for a sleigh ride?"

"Does the entire Thorley house party go?"

His mouth curved with tenderness. "No. Do you not trust me?"

To be honest it was actually herself she did not trust. Common sense seemed to flee in his presence. Replaced by a delirium that ate away at her brain, urging her to jump into an abyss.

She recalled the ecstasy of being held against his hard body and his kisses that had thrilled her. Trapped by her own emotions, Dorie inhaled deeply and stepped off the ledge. "Very well."

He gently kissed her hand, his breath warm on her skin. He looked at her from beneath hooded lashes. "Until this afternoon." Then he turned and was gone.

Her attention slowly returned to reality and Dorie became aware of Hannah's scrutiny. Eyes wide and luminous, Hannah asked, "perhaps he plans to propose marriage."

"No, Hannah. You must not believe I will gain a husband simply because you asked your angel."

"But it's Christmas Eve! Miracles always happen after midnight."

Dorie bit back bitter laughter. Her sister thought it would take a miracle for her to find a husband. And she was probably right. At twenty-seven years, she was firmly on the shelf. Certainly not to be dusted off by Ash.

Dorie stood. "I should start the baking."

"Will we wear our new dresses tonight?" Rose asked from the doorway.

"We shall wear them tomorrow." Dorie forced a

smile and retreated to the kitchen, confident the baking would relieve her mind from torturous thoughts, but could not halt her ponderings of dark eyes and warm lips.

The chilled air fluttered over her as the horse trotted along the road, pulling the sleigh. The countryside faded into a blur. Aware only of the man beside her emanating a roaring heat and the scent of the outdoors.

Strong, sure hands handled the reins with ease and confidence. Warmth burned her face as she remembered those same hands touching her so intimately. It seemed a lifetime ago that she had been concerned only with knitting and caring for Hannah and Aunt Rose. Now, visions of Ash permeated her mind and the unique way he touched her.

"It looks like it may snow tonight," Ash murmured.

His warm breath tickled her ear and Dorie shivered. Inane words, yet the deep voice that evoked them swirled over her, dangerous and seductive. "Yes."

His arm circled her shoulders and pulled her against him. "Are you warm enough?"

Nodding, she snuggled into his side, her heart thumping a frenzied beat. The setting sun shimmered on the field of snow.

Limbs now bare of their leaves stretched toward the sky, adorned only with snow and ice. Directing the horse and sleigh into the copse of oaks, Ash said, "I want to show you something."

He halted the horse and vaulted onto the ground.

Turning, Ash clasped her waist and swung her down. Hands continued to circle her waist and he stared into her eyes, his own fathomless pools of polished black. Squeezing her waist lightly, he tucked her hand in the crook of his arm and led her down the embankment.

Through the shadows of the trees wound a brook encrusted with snow and ice, but still the water flowed on its course—only hindered, not paralyzed by the weather. The quiet surrounded them. It was as if they were the only two people in existence.

Ash halted and pointed to the stream bank. "Here we are. I've never seen snowflakes bloom in December."

In the loose soil of the riverbank sprouted the delicate blossoms, their white bell-shaped heads bent as if in prayer.

"Nor have I. Hannah would call this a miracle." Dorie crouched and brushed the flowers with her fingertips. It was amazing that something so fragile defied the harsh winter.

A baying hovered in the air. Dorie shivered and stood, pressing closer to Ash. "W-was that a wolf?"

His arm encircled her waist. "Yes. We best get back to the horse."

They trudged back to the copse of oaks where they had alighted from the sleigh. Dorie turned in a complete circle, her mouth gaping open. "Where is he?"

Ash sighed. "It appears as if our horse has abandoned us."

"But did you not tie the reins to a tree?" she demanded.

The tips of Ash's ears turned red. "I believe I may have neglected that chore."

Dorie rolled her eyes. "Wonderful! Now we shall have to walk all the way back to Thorley House."

Ash shook his head. "It is too far in this cold and dark will descend soon. There is an abandoned cottage not far from here. We can take shelter there until Thor sends people searching for us."

"You think they'll send searchers?"

"Once the horse and sleigh reaches the stable, the stable master will inform Thor of our absence. He will organize a search party straightaway."

"Do you think the wolf frightened the horse?"

"Most likely." Ash's arm circled her waist. "Do not worry. You are safe."

A smile tugged at the corner of her mouth. "I know. Now shall you lead me to our shelter?"

A deep chuckle answered her, and he bowed in a chivalrous manner. "Very well, my lady." Lacing his fingers with hers, Ash led her to the road.

Orange and pink painted the sky as the sun sank into the horizon. Pine and oncoming snow scented the evening air.

"Did you mean for us to be abandoned?" Dorie asked.

"No!"

"You seem to have a talent for getting stranded."

"Dorie, I am sorry for landing us in this state of affairs. Not only will you be cold, but hungry. You shall miss most of the gaiety of Christmas Eve."

Dorie squeezed his hand. "I do not care so much for my sake, but Hannah will be sorely disappointed to miss it all."

"I made arrangements with Thor's servants for Hannah and Rose to be brought to Thorley House."

Dorie halted and stared at Ash. "You did?"

Ash nodded. "I planned to keep you out as long as possible." His words were filled with a heavy dose of self-mockery and apprehension of her reaction.

A warm glow flowed through her, but she strained to control the outward show of her emotions. Under his dark scrutiny, she stared at the snow-covered road. "Really?" she finally managed to say. Even to her own ears, her voice was a breathy whisper.

He tugged her to a halt and with a finger to her chin, gently forced her head up. Wary eyes searched her face.

The wealth and title he was born into had instilled poise and aplomb in the man. For the first time in their short acquaintance, Ash displayed a chink in his armor of self-confidence and appeared to require assurances.

Dorie brushed her gloved fingers over his cheek. "Do not fret. I lay no anger on you."

A grin overtook his features and his gaze softened. Kissing her hand, he said, "The cottage is not far now. We'll build a fire to drive the cold from our bones."

His words were true. Only a few feet ahead they came upon the cottage. The disrepair and neglect were remarkable. The door, minus a hinge, hung half off the doorjamb. Panes of glass of the windows were shattered. Debris littered the walkway and doorstep. Ash picked up several sticks and limbs that were not wet with snow. "At least I can get a fire started with these."

With caution, they picked their way through the

disarray. Ash grunted as he shoved the door back enough to allow them to slip through.

"Stay near the door until I get a fire going," he instructed. Flint struck and a branch caught fire. Ash held it up to survey the room. "Ah, here's the fireplace."

The stale smell of dust and mold attacked Dorie's nose and she sneezed.

"I'll have the fire going in a moment so you can warm yourself."

Dorie sniffed and said, "I think it is the dust making me sneeze." She wiggled her toes and fingers, stiff with cold.

He stacked the wood in the fireplace and set flame to it. The wood crackled and popped.

Spiderwebs danced in the breeze. Disintegrating chairs and broken glass cluttered the small room. "We can use the chairs for firewood," Dorie noted.

Nodding, Ash piled pieces on the fire. Dorie searched around, finding an old counterpane. She shook the old rag out and laid it in front of the fireplace.

Ash rose and said, "We should have enough wood for the fire."

"Do you think it will take Thor long to start searching?" Holding her hands out to the fire, Dorie warmed them.

"To start the search, no. It may be a while before they find us, however."

"One should keep watch, lest they pass us by."

"I am certain Thor is aware of all the possible shelters on his land. They will check those first."

Taking her hand, Ash led Dorie to the counterpane. "We might as well be as comfortable as our surroundings will allow."

Sitting down, Dorie was paralyzed for a moment, uncertain of what to say or do. Being so alone with Ash made her nerves jitter. It could take their rescuers hours to find them. What in the world would they talk of? Tension burgeoned in her stomach like a lead ball, heavy and tight, and her shoulders ached with strain.

Dorie searched her mind to come up with a topic of conversation. "When do you go to confront the man who bought the items stolen from Thor and Bella?"

A knowing smile spread across his face. "In three or four days. You do not have to try so hard to talk."

Heat flushed Dorie's face. "What makes you think that?"

Ash shrugged. "It is as if I can hear the gears churning in your brain." Pitching his hat to the side, he lay back and closed his eyes. "You may wish to rest. The night may be long."

Dorie removed her bonnet and kneaded her neck to loosen the tense muscles. It was ridiculous to feel so apprehensive. After all, she trusted Ash with her very life. He would never harm her.

She glanced at him, but his eyes were still closed, serene and quiet. Maybe even asleep.

Bit by bit, Dorie reclined. Still, Ash had not moved. She breathed a sigh of relief. Closing her eyes, Dorie allowed herself to relax and drowsiness overtook her.

She fought through the cobwebs of sleep and opened her eyes to find herself disoriented and be-

A GIFT OF LOVE 211

wildered. Her bed was hard and uncomfortable, but a warmth surrounded her.

A deep voice whispered in her ear, "So, you are finally awake."

Twenty-one

Sensing her nervousness earlier, Ash had closed his eyes, hoping she would relax. Apparently, sleep had claimed them both.

While they slept, she had pillowed her head on his shoulder and he had wrapped his arms tightly around her. It had been agony watching her sleep for almost half an hour. Silky hair had tickled his nose and the scent of roses had permeated his senses. He wondered if she had any idea of the torment that holding her created. Now the heavy lashes that shadowed her cheeks flew up and she stiffened within his arms.

"Did you have a nice nap?" he asked, nuzzling her neck. She smelled fresh and sweet. Of roses.

"Y-yes," she replied, and tried to pull away. He held on, not yet ready to relinquish his hold of her, the prolonged anticipation almost unbearable. An intense physical awareness of this woman had presented itself the first time he laid eyes on her, and it had not lessened over time as he had expected. If anything, the attraction grew more powerful with time, and he was tired of battling the wisdom of relinquishing the attraction.

Dorie's uneven breathing fanned his ear. She was as affected as he. But she was an innocent, his conscience asserted. He forced the thought away. Nothing mattered except claiming her in the way only a man can claim a woman. To satisfy his burning desire, his aching need.

His lips brushed against hers as he spoke. "Dorie, tell me now if you want me to stop, or I shall not be able to."

She stared at him, her blue eyes wide and luminous, filled with mystery and yearning. His thumb caressed her cheek.

Her answer was to press her lips to his and bury her fingers in his hair, shattering the small fragment of calm he had managed to hang onto. Ash needed no further encouragement. He devoured the softness of her lips. Forcing them open with his thrusting tongue, he delved inside, consumed by the taste of her.

Rolling his hard body atop hers, he crushed her into the counterpane. Her softness and heat were discernible even through their layers of clothing.

With trembling fingers, he unbuttoned her coat and threw it aside. Unfastening the tapes of her gown, he pushed the gown's bodice and her chemise down to her waist. She shivered as his eyes boldly absorbed the sight of her bare breasts. He murmured, "Beautiful," and his tongue caressed a swollen nipple.

Dorie moaned and her body arched toward him, yearning for more, imprisoning him in a web of desire and arousal.

A thought skittered through his mind that he should stop his seduction. This bewitching minx was different. But he forced the thought aside. He must claim her.

Ash stood and quickly shed his clothes and boots. Wide blue eyes watched his every movement. Dorie's face flushed as she beheld his full arousal. He smiled at her. "All will be well. Trust me."

Dorie nodded and gasped as he pulled her gown, chemise, shoes, and stockings off. His gaze drank in the beautiful sight of her as the glow of the crackling fire rippled over soft ivory flesh. Coming down on top of her, he gathered her against his pulsating body. She gasped in sweet agony as bare chest met bare chest, soft breasts and feminine heat crushed against him.

He wished to take the time to explore, to arouse every inch of her, but their rescuers could arrive at any time. It would be disastrous to be discovered in the act of making love to her. Unfortunately their time alone would compromise her no matter how innocent their togetherness.

Soft fingers trailed up and down his back. Ash gritted his teeth and attempted to control his surging blood. He wanted nothing more than to sink himself into her wet heat, but he must grant her a little more time.

Erratic emotions stormed through Dorie as Ash wove a spell entwining her in his magic. His tongue licked her nipple, taut with desire, and the breast tingled against the large, callused hand that caressed it.

The truth had been evident to her for days. She loved Ash and could not deny herself his touch. She welcomed each memory of him.

His fingers slid over her stomach to her most feminine core and her thoughts scattered into a million fragments. A pressure began to coil inside her, winding tighter and tighter as he stroked her.

"Ash . . ." she whispered, unsure of the extraordinary exhilaration he generated.

"Trust me."

A tremor of fiery sensations flooded through her and she moaned in sweet agony as her body vibrated and shuddered against him. He did not give her turbulent passion time to recede.

Her breath caught in her throat as he slowly filled her. Sweat beaded his forehead and back. He plunged forward and pain tore through her. She bit her bottom lip to forestall the cry that welled up.

He stilled and lay his forehead against hers. "Forgive me. The pain will be short-lived."

For a moment, Dorie wondered if the pleasure was worth the pain. Then the ache began to subside, replaced by a reawakened desire.

"Better?"

"Yes," she whispered, then giggled.

Ash frowned. "What the devil are you giggling about?"

"Remembering my näiveté when I thought an animal burrowed in your clothes . . . and what I almost cudgeled."

Ash smiled. "I am glad you did not use the fire iron and spoil this moment." He nibbled on her earlobe and fondled her breast. She trembled against him.

"I wish I had all night," he whispered, and began to stroke in and out. The now-familiar pressure coiled in her again. Dark hot hunger radiated from his eyes.

Never had she dreamed of the bliss of his passion. The joy that came with the man she loved possessing her as no other.

Ash thrust against her once more, and pure, explosive pleasure spiraled through her again. Ash went rigid and groaned her name. Ecstasy burst through her.

An amazing sense of completeness permeated her being and she savored the satisfaction.

Ash buried his face in her neck and gathered her against his warm, pulsing body. He gulped in great drafts of air. "My sweet Dorie," he whispered.

A horrible thought entered her mind. How did she compare to the other women he had made love to? Was he disappointed in her abilities?

In the distance the church tenor bell began to toll. The bell would sound the number of years since Christ's birth. The last chime would coincide with the first stroke of midnight.

She had missed the Christmas Eve festivities, but did not regret it. This evening would remain in her memory forever. The night Ash had possessed her and for a moment, however brief, they had belonged to one another.

Her hands caressed the strong planes of his back, still damp from their lovemaking. The world consisted only of him. She succumbed to the sleep of a satisfied lover.

Shouts filtered through the passionate haze. Ash rose and looked out the window. "Best get ready to meet our searchers."

The hour of reckoning had arrived. Though

numbed with sleep, Dorie jumped up and quickly dressed. Heat flushed her face as she stared at the blood-stained counterpane. She folded the cloth and secreted it in a dark corner.

She turned back to find Ash dressed and looking as polished as if he had just left his valet.

It was too much to hope that no one knew of the hours she had been alone with Ash. Her reputation could go to the devil. She would never marry because she had been compromised. Not that Ash had mentioned marriage once.

Dorie looked at Ash. He stood before the fire, hands clasped behind his back, his face a blank mask. She would have given anything to know what his thoughts were.

The door swung open and bounced against the wall. "Damnation, I thought we would never find you!" Thor exclaimed. "Are either of you hurt?"

Ash answered, "No, and we managed to keep warm with the fire."

Thor stuck his head out the door. Torches glowed over the men and horses outside. "Fire the gun. We finally found them." Turning back to Dorie, he said, "The carriage will be here in a few moments."

"I suppose everyone knows we have been together?" Dorie murmured.

Thor sighed. "Yes, I'm afraid there was no way to keep it quiet."

Dorie shrugged and laughed. "Well, it is not as if my reputation was of any use to me here in our small village."

Thor glanced at Ash as if expecting him to say something, but no words were forthcoming. A muscle ticked in Thor's jaw. "Step outside with me, Ash."

"No."

"Do you really wish me to embarrass Dorie by saying what I have to say in front of her?"

"I have no desire for you to embarrass Dorie, nor to hear anything you must say in private."

Through gritted teeth, Thor seethed, "Very well, Lord Ashborne." He turned and stormed out into the night.

Dorie's stomach twisted and churned. She suspected that their tiff involved her.

"Ash . . ." The rattle of carriage wheels interrupted her.

He broke his vigil by the fireplace. Shepherding her to the door, he said, "We best be on our way."

"But Ash . . ."

Cold eyes met hers. "Now is not the time to stand about talking."

Dorie shivered and nodded. She wrapped her arms around herself and blinked back tears. *I will not cry.*

Heavy silence weighed down on Dorie, cutting off her breath as the carriage conveyed her and Ash back to Thorley Park. She must wait until she was alone before she allowed her misery rein.

Torches and lanterns lit Thorley Park as the carriage approached, making the estate warm and inviting; but it did not drive away Dorie's coldness.

She ignored the helping hand Ash extended and bounded down on her own. Bella awaited them in the doorway, concern etched on her face. Taking

A GIFT OF LOVE

Dorie's hands in hers, she squeezed them. "Are you well?"

Dorie forced a smile. "Yes. We were able to build a fire to keep warm. I believe I should retire home."

"I have already made arrangements for you, Rose, and Hannah to spend the night. Rose and a footman have already gathered the necessities from your cottage. I insist you have a sip of brandy and I imagine you are starving." Bella untied Dorie's bonnet and unbuttoned her coat while Ash removed his own coat and hat. Placing an arm around her shoulders, Bella steered her toward the drawing room.

"Not really."

"Nonetheless, you shall eat a little something."

"Has everyone retired?"

"Not everyone. We were very worried about you. Being abandoned could have been trecherous in this weather."

Conversation lulled in the drawing room as every eye turned to the foursome entering the room. Vanora's eyes were huge as she stared at Dorie.

Rose jumped up and rushed to Dorie. Throwing her arms around her, Rose said, "We were so very worried about you. I am so glad to see you are well."

Dorie hugged her. "A good night's rest and I will be as good as new."

Rose drew back and studied Dorie's face. "You're certain you are well?"

Dorie nodded. "Where is Hannah?"

"In bed."

Bella tugged Dorie over to the settee and Thor placed a snifter of brandy in her hand and one in Ash's. Dorie sipped it, then coughed as the brandy burned its way down her throat.

In a superfluous whisper to Lady Marwood, Mrs. Peters said, "It is most unfortunate his lordship has compromised such a lamentable creature."

Embarrassment burned Dorie's cheeks and she stared at her lap.

Black chips of ice froze in his eyes and Ash chastised, "Madam, I will thank you not to speak of my betrothed in such a manner."

Twenty-two

Lady Marwood gasped and Bella clapped her hands in glee.

With difficulty, Dorie contained her surprise and shock. Betrothed! The man possessed a lot of nerve to call her his betrothed when he had not bothered to speak with her. But she did not want to create a scene, so she held her tongue for the moment. She would ring a peal over his head when they were alone.

Mrs. Peters inclined her head. "I beg your pardon, my lord."

Barrett entered. "Lord Ashborne, Miss Knighton, your dinner is set up in the dining room."

Dorie breathed a silent sigh of relief and placed her glass on the side table. "Thank you, Barrett."

Ash rose and extended his arm to Dorie. She hesitated a moment, then laid her hand on his sleeve and allowed him to lead her to the dining room.

From the food laid out on the sideboard, Dorie chose mutton, bread, cheese, and an apple. She slipped into a chair, knowing the food would taste like sawdust. Once Ash sat and dismissed the servants, he turned to her as if awaiting her reaction.

"You should not have lied to everyone," she reproached him.

"And when did I lie?" he asked in a soft voice.

"When you said we were betrothed."

"I assumed we were after I compromised you."

"We both know you do not marry every woman you . . . you . . ." Heat flushed her face.

A brow arched. "Yes?"

She sighed and whispered, "Every woman you are intimate with."

"But then, you are my first virtuous woman."

Her mouth gaped open and he frowned at her. " 'Tis the truth."

"I will not be married simply because everyone thinks me compromised."

"Thinks?"

"No one knows the truth of what did or did not occur. I do not go about in society and a ruined reputation is no great loss."

"And if you are with child?"

"But it was only once."

"Once is all it takes."

Dorie stared at her plate. "Still, I will not be married out of hand."

His voice softened, cajoling. "Dorie, be reasonable."

She threw her serviette onto the table and pounced up, her chair falling backwards. "If that is your idea of being reasonable, no!" Dorie fled from the room.

Ash sighed and gulped his wine.

Bella inquired from the door, "What is wrong with Dorie?"

"She takes exception to my marrying her."

"Did you tell her you love her when you proposed?"

Ash stared at his wineglass and twirled the crystal between his fingers.

"You did speak to her before your announcement, didn't you?"

"No."

"Ash!" Bella's voice was filled with censure. "How could you?"

"I assumed she expected the appropriate deed of me after she has been compromised."

Bella rolled her eyes and muttered, "Men!"

Ash cleared his throat and the tips of his ears burned. "Bella, how do I change her mind?"

"You're not relieved she refused you?"

"Of course not." His voice became a whisper. "She may carry my child."

"Is that the only reason?"

"What do you want me to say?"

"The truth of your feelings. Do you love her?"

"I-I suppose." He looked at Bella. "I am not certain I know what love is."

Bella smiled and patted his hand. "How do you feel and what do you think when she is with you and when she is not?"

"When she is not with me, I wish her by my side. When she is by my side, I find it difficult not to touch her." Ash shrugged. "I wish her happiness more than anything."

"Sounds like love to me."

Hope stirred and Ash stared at Bella. "But I do not know how she feels about me."

"I have known Dorie many years. She would never give herself to a man unless she loved him."

"I suppose I should go to her and confess my feelings."

Bella grimaced and clutched her stomach.

Ash came to his feet. "Bella?"

"I'm well. I have been experiencing a few pains this evening."

"Good Lord, have you told Thor?" he demanded.

"No, he would only hover. I'm waiting until the time is close."

"Damnation!" he muttered.

"And you will not tell him either."

"Bella . . ."

"Promise me, Ash." She squeezed the chair arms as another pain apparently cut through her.

He knelt beside her and clasped one hand in his. "Bella my dear, we must send for the doctor immediately."

"No! It could be hours."

"But Bella . . ."

"What is this?" Thor demanded from the doorway.

Bella smiled, but it was sickly at best. "Ash was just thanking me for my counsel." Green eyes dared him to contradict her.

Ash sighed and stood. "She has been most helpful. I shall bid you both good night."

Thor laid his hand on Ash's shoulder. "I do not want to sound patronizing, but I'm proud you plan to do the right thing by Dorie."

Ash smiled. "Now, I just have to convince Dorie to accept me." He spun around, leaving Thor staring after him.

***

A GIFT OF LOVE

Dorie stared into the mirror. Christmas morning had emerged bright and clear, but she was looking dull and haggard. Dark circles shadowed her eyes and her heart was heavy.

Marrying the man she loved should have overjoyed her, but Ash was following convention rather than his heart.

A hand tapped at the door. "Come in," Dorie called, wondering who it could be.

Hannah entered, dressed in her new gown. Excitement glittered in her eyes. Dorie smiled. "You look beautiful. Happy birthday."

Hannah grinned and hugged Dorie. "Aunt Rose told me you and Ash would be married."

Dorie led Hannah to sit on the edge of the bed. Holding Hannah's hands, Dorie explained, "That is not quite true."

A frown marred Hannah's face.

"You see, Hannah, Ash only announced our engagement because we were stranded together last night. If I were to marry, it would be because I loved the man, not because society whispered about me."

"You don't love Ash?" Hannah asked, clearly unbelieving.

Dorie sighed. She could not lie. "Yes, I love Ash, but he does not love me. So I cannot marry him. Now, tell me about the festivities last night. Were they wonderful?"

"Oh, yes! Carolers came by singing and wassail was passed around. Lord Thorley lit the candles on the huge kissing bough and kissed Lady Thorley under it. Then, with my help, he lit the yule log and we played charades and bullet pudding."

Dorie laughed at her joy. "And who was the unlucky one who had to dig the bullet from the flour without using their hands?"

Hannah giggled. "Lord Thorley. He had flour all over himself. He looked like a ghost." Hannah's face grew serious. "I was disappointed you and Ash were not here."

Dorie squeezed her hand. "Me, too. I wished I had spent Christmas Eve with you."

Hannah's face brightened. "But we have Christmas."

"You look quite wonderful in your new gown. I'm afraid you shall have to wait until we return home to receive your birthday present from Aunt Rose and me."

"I don't mind. Today is going to be wonderful."

"Why don't you go see Aunt Rose while I dress. We shall be leaving for the church service soon."

Nodding, Hannah kissed Dorie's cheek. "Very well."

Emptiness pervaded Dorie's being. Once again alone, Dorie pushed her thoughts away from Ash and girded herself with resolve to face him and show no panic.

But would this change his vow to clear Aunt Rose?

Ash waited while his valet brushed his coat and studied himself in the mirror. He looked as if he had not slept well last night, and in fact he had not.

A knock sounded at the door. Pemberton opened the door and stared down his nose. His voice filled with condescension, he said, "His lordship cannot see you presently."

A GIFT OF LOVE 227

"Please, Mr. Pemberton, it is very important," Hannah pleaded softly.

"Allow her entrance, Pemberton," Ash said.

Hannah entered, her head hanging, her eyes downcast. "I'm sorry to bother you."

"That will be all, Pemberton." The valet bowed and departed.

Kneeling on one knee, Ash took her hand and kissed it. "No bother at all, my dear. I am pleased to see you. Did you enjoy Christmas Eve?" Placing a finger under her chin, he raised her face.

She smiled. "Yes, it was quite wonderful. I-I wish you and Dorie had been present."

"So do I, little one. But we have today and there is always next year."

"Perhaps I will not see you next year," Hannah whispered.

"I doubt that since you will be living with me."

"Dorie says she won't marry you because you don't love her."

"Suppose you leave your sister to me and trust me to change her mind about marriage."

"Dorie is awfully stubborn," Hannah whispered.

A hearty chuckle struggled through Ash's frown. "So am I. Trust me?"

Hannah nodded.

Standing, Ash walked to the armoire and picked up a package wrapped in silver and red. "Happy birthday, angel."

Hannah's mouth gaped in surprise. "You bought me a birthday present."

"Of course." Ash led her to the settee. "Shall you open it now?"

Hannah's hand reverently touched the red ribbon. "It's too pretty to unwrap."

"That is no fun," Ash declared. "Rip it open."

Hannah slowly untied the ribbon and lifted the lid. She gasped. "Oh, Ash, she is beautiful," Hannah declared with awe, and lifted the doll.

"I was not certain what you would enjoy for your birthday. I realize this angel is not male, but she looked like she needed a good home."

Hannah stroked the doll's gown of white silk shot with silver threads. Painted blue eyes gazed upon her new owner. A halo shimmered on blond hair fashioned into ringlets.

Ash smiled. Apparently, he had chosen well. The expense and trouble of having the angel doll made in such a short time was worth it for Hannah's look of awe.

Hannah gently laid the doll on the bed and threw her arms around Ash. "An angel from my angel. I'll give her a very good home, Ash."

Brushing Hannah's hair, Ash said, "I know you will. But I am not an angel. Now I suppose we should go downstairs."

"May I leave her here until we return from church?"

Ash nodded.

Hannah gently smoothed the doll's gown and place her hand in Ash's.

The Christmas worshipers meandered down the church aisle after the late morning service of carols and sermon. Spirals of ivy circled the pillars, and lanterns of evergreen hung from the arches.

A GIFT OF LOVE 229

Bella strolled beside Dorie. Bella came to an abrupt halt and stopped breathing as well. Then she inhaled deeply. "Bella, are you ill?" Dorie asked.

Bella shook her head and kneaded her back. "Give me your arm."

Dorie held out her arm and Bella clasped it. Walking again, Bella whispered, "I believe my time draws near."

"And Thor allowed you to attend church service?" Dorie asked in disbelief.

Bella grinned sheepishly. "I have not told him exactly."

"Exactly what have you told him?" Dorie demanded.

Bella shrugged. "Nothing."

"Nothing?" Dorie shouted.

"Shhh! You shall have Thor asking what is wrong," Bella cautioned.

"And well he should know."

Bella shook her head. "I do not intend for him to know until the last possible moment."

"Bella, I do not think that is wise."

"Nonetheless, that is my choice and you shall *not* tell him." Green eyes pleaded with her.

"Bella . . ."

"I do not want Thor to know!" Bella said between gritted teeth.

Dorie sighed and rolled her eyes. "You are as stubborn as a mule."

Bella smiled. "Very true, but I will not have Thor hovering and worrying until absolutely necessary. If it were possible, I would have this child without his knowing until afterward."

"That is as impossible as preventing the sun's rising each morning."

"Yes, and that is why you must keep my counsel. I shall strive to make it through Christmas Day before giving birth."

Laughter bubbled up and Dorie said, "Nature will decide when your child is born, not yourself. You may birth this baby during Christmas dinner."

"I wish to speak of something else," Bella informed her. "Let us talk of your wedding."

Dorie frowned. "There will be no wedding for me."

"Even after he compromised you?"

Dorie shook her head.

"Because you think he does not love you."

"You know the truth also. I cannot blame him. If I am truthful, I must admit I allowed myself to be seduced."

"I said *think,* Dorie. He does love you."

Dorie snorted and their conversation drew to a close as they joined Lord Thorley and the other houseguests awaiting the carriages.

Dorie swallowed hard, lifted her chin, forced a demure smile, and boldly met Ash's gaze. Cold dignity created a stone mask of his face. Lethal determination and unspoken promises glittered in his black eyes.

Twenty-three

The dinner table shimmered with red, green, and gold. Holly and ivy overflowed the epergnes. Tension thick enough to cut with a knife sat at the table as if a guest.

Thomas asked, "So, Miss Knighton, when will you and my dear cousin wed?"

Taking a bite of goose, Dorie said, "We have not discussed a date as of yet." She looked across at Ash. "Have we, my lord?"

Ash smiled. "No, but I suspect it will not be too long. I never favored a long engagement."

Dorie bit back the words that came to her lips. This engagement would last longer than he preferred. Forever, in fact. Everyone would depart Thorley Park after Twelfth Night. Let them think the engagement stood. They would discover soon enough that she had not wed Ash.

Thomas glanced at Rose. "I suppose you shall wait until the matter of the thefts is settled."

Ash sipped his wine. "I expect that truth to be known very soon."

"Really?" Thomas asked, eyebrows raised in surprise. "How is that, cousin?"

"I prefer not to disclose the information I have discovered. But as I knew, Rose is innocent."

"Then why was my diamond brooch discovered in her possession?" Lady Marwood asked in disdain.

"The real thief secreted it there to throw suspicion on Rose and away from himself."

"Himself? But could it not be a woman as well?" Bella asked.

Ash smiled. "Of course. We shall know the truth in a few days."

Silverware clattered on china. Bella clutched the table edge and squeezed her eyes tight.

Thor's chair thumped back to the floor as he sprang up and stared across the table at his wife. "Bella?" he roared.

"I-I believe my . . . water has broken," she whispered.

Thor stalked to her side and scooped her up in his arms. "Send a missive to the doctor immediately and send Bella's maid to her bedchamber," he instructed a footman.

Bella whispered, "Dorie, please come with me."

Dorie followed Thor up the stairs, aware that Ash followed behind her. Rushing to the bed, Dorie jerked the covers down and Thor gently laid Bella in the bed. Bella forced a smile. "Gentlemen, please leave us a moment."

"No!" Thor roared.

"Just until I get into a nightdress. Please, Thor," Bella pleaded.

"Very well," he acquiesced, but was clearly unhappy about it.

Bella sat on the edge of the bed and the maid undressed her while Dorie searched through the ar-

A GIFT OF LOVE 233

moire for a nightdress. Finding one, Dorie turned back to the bed and slipped the linen garment over Bella's head.

Bella clenched her teeth together in pain, then, breathed deeply. "Please loose my hair, Dulcie."

"Yes, ma'am."

Dulcie quickly removed the pins from Bella's hair and Dorie brushed it. "Would you like a ribbon to tie it back?" Dorie asked.

"Not presently," Bella answered, and slipped her legs under the covers. "On your way out, Dulcie, let Thor back in."

She curtsied. "Yes, my lady."

Thor stormed in and leaned over the bed. "Well?" he demanded.

Bella's eyes narrowed. "It shall require a little more time than this. If you are going to be a pest, you may leave now." She pointed toward the door.

His face softened and he took her hand. "I promise not to vex you. I only ask you wait for the doctor's arrival."

"We shall see. Now, sit down somewhere and allow Dorie to wash my face with a wet cloth."

Thor traversed to the window, muttering, "Tyrannical woman," then bellowed, "Ash, come talk to me."

Sitting on the bed's edge, Dorie bathed Bella's face with a cool cloth. Bella blew out puffs of breath.

Dorie gently chastised, "You should not have waited so long to send for the doctor."

"Possibly," Bella reluctantly agreed. "I am sorry you are missing Christmas dinner."

Dorie smiled. "I am certain Cook will save us

some food. Perhaps you would like your mother with you."

"Damnation, no. She will be of no comfort to me." Bella squeezed Dorie's hand as another pain struck her. After a moment, she released Dorie's hand and breathed deeply. "I apologize for asking you to attend me. After all, you are unmarried, but no one else would soothe me."

"I do not mind. It shall be as close as I will come to motherhood."

Bella's brows rose. "You think so?"

Dorie nodded.

Bella glanced at Thor and Ash. Then she whispered, "Ash means to change your mind."

"That is not possible. Now, is there anything I can do to make you more comfortable?" Dorie fluffed her pillow.

Bella sighed and said, "Water."

Dorie poured water into a glass and held it to Bella's lips. She sipped, and then her head dropped back onto the pillow. "I am not so certain I wish to have a child," Bella announced, then suddenly scowled and gritted her teeth.

Dorie settled into the chair beside the bed. "It is a little late for that decision."

Bella shouted, "The cold in this room would freeze a witch's teat, Thor! Stoke up the fire."

Muttering under his breath, Thor did as ordered. Shortly, the fire blazed and crackled.

Dorie whispered, "You should thank him."

Bella snorted. "My condition is his fault. He can damn well pay for it." She clenched her teeth again and grimaced. "I think the pains are coming closer together."

"Where the devil is that doctor?" Thor demanded, his voice harsh and piercing.

Pacing over to the bed, Thor shook his finger at Bella. "You will wait for the doctor's arrival to have this baby."

Grimacing in pain, Bella said, "Try telling that to your son or daughter. He or she may be as impatient as you."

"Thor, perhaps you would like to go back down to dinner," Dorie suggested.

Narrowed eyes stared at her. "Not likely."

"Then I suggest you keep any forthcoming comments to yourself," Dorie stated. "So far, they have not been helpful."

Bella cackled in glee. "You tell him! Men are quite inconsiderate."

Rolling his eyes, Thor retreated to the window and in a hushed tone spoke to Ash. Amusement twitched at Ash's mouth, but he managed to restrain his mirth.

"You should be ashamed," Dorie gently chastised.

"Wait until it's your turn. See how considerate you feel like being."

A timid knock sounded. Thor rushed across and flung the door open. His shoulders collapsed in dismay. Instead of the doctor he obviously expected, he discovered Hannah.

Eyes downcast, she asked, "May I speak to Lady Thorley?"

"She is busy at the moment, Hannah . . ."

Bella bellowed, "Allow the child to come in."

Opening the door wide, Thor bowed and gestured with his hand for Hannah to enter. Hannah shuffled over to the bed. "I'm sorry to bother you, Lady

Thorley, but I thought you might need a good luck charm."

Hannah opened her hand to reveal a silver angel. "Mama possessed this when she delivered me ten years ago on Christmas Day. She said it gave her great comfort."

Bella accepted the angel and smiled. "Thank you, Hannah. I am certain it will soothe me."

Dorie gently pushed her toward the door. "Run along now and enjoy the Christmas festivities."

Bella fingered the angel and said, "It appears my child shall be born on Christmas Day with his or her very own Christmas angel. What exactly do Christmas angels do?"

Ash strolled over. "They protect the child."

"A guardian angel?"

Ash nodded. "Then, on the child's tenth birthday any wishes are granted as long as they are unselfish."

"Ash! That is ridiculous!" Dorie exclaimed.

"Well, I saw Hannah's letter and every wish she made has come true."

Dorie's fingers drummed a staccato beat on the chair arm. "There is yet one not answered and it will remain so. I control the outcome of that one."

Ash's mouth curved with tenderness. "Do not be too certain." Ignoring her icy stare, he turned and rejoined Thor at the window.

Annoyance devoured her. Of all the unmitigated gall! She clasped her shaking hands together in her lap and ignored Bella's snort of amusement.

Knowing Ash was with Lord Thorley, Hannah charged into his room, anxious to retrieve her angel.

A GIFT OF LOVE 237

She clutched the most beautiful doll she had ever seen to her chest.

The door between the bedchamber and sitting room squeaked open. Turning, Hannah was confronted with a malefactor clutching Ash's diamond stickpin and money.

"What are you doing with Ash's belongings?" she demanded.

Surprise dawned and narrowed eyes probed her. "What are you doing here, little girl?"

"Retrieving my doll. You're the thief," Hannah whispered.

The intruder stepped closer to her. "You should not bother your pretty little head with an adult's affair."

Fear squeezed her heart. For the first time, Hannah realized what a precarious position she was in. The miscreant could hurt her and no one would ever know what happened.

Hannah inhaled deeply and dashed for the door, her only thought to find a place to hide. The only trustworthy people were in Lady Thorley's bedchamber, and they were much too busy.

Stalking footsteps treaded on the stairs behind her. Labored breathing filled her ears. Fingers of dread raced up her spine.

Twenty-four

The long case clock in the hall bonged. Dorie mentally counted the chimes. Nine o'clock.

The doctor had finally arrived, but was now downstairs waiting for the delivery time to approach closer. Thor and Ash sat in front of the fireplace sipping brandy. Sweat beaded Bella's face, her eyes closed in agony. Once again Dorie bathed Bella's face with a cold, wet cloth.

Through gritted teeth, Bella said, "I believe Thor can give birth to our next child."

"I am certain he would if it were possible," Dorie replied.

Bella snorted. "Hardly. Men are such babies. They could never withstand the pain."

"How many times must she mock me?" Thor asked Ash. "Do all women insult their husbands during childbirth?"

"I'm certain she does not mean the things she has said," Ash replied.

Bella snorted again. "I mean every damn word."

Dorie said, "You know that is not so, Bella. I have never seen anyone who loves her husband as much as you love Thor."

A GIFT OF LOVE

"I do not feel very loving presently," Bella retorted. "As a matter of fact, Thor's loving days are over. Never again!"

Walking to the fireplace, Dorie laid her hand on Thor's shoulder. "Pay her words no heed. They will be forgotten in the joy of motherhood."

"One can hope. Where is that blasted doctor?" Thor demanded.

"Downstairs partaking of Cook's cake and coffee." Dorie warmed her hands at the fire.

"He ought to be up here," Thor asserted, and paced over to the bed. "How are you, dear heart?" Thor clasped Bella's hand and kissed it.

"I'm fine, darling. I'm anxious to hold our son or daughter."

"But . . . the pain?"

Bella smiled at him. "Having our child will be worth every pang."

Rising from his chair, Ash stood beside Dorie. "Charming, aren't they?"

"Yes."

Ash dropped to one knee and clasped Dorie's hand. "I love you, Dorie. Will you do me the honor of becoming my wife?"

Shock washed over Dorie. "You-you do not mean that," she whispered.

Black eyes radiated passion and promises. "I would not make such a vow unless it were the truth. I thought mayhap you returned my feelings. After last night, can you honestly tell me you do not love me?"

"But . . ."

"Dorie!" Thor shouted. "Bella needs you."

Dorie smiled wistfully and brushed Ash's cheek with her fingers. She returned to the bedside.

Bella's eyes squeezed shut as a pain obviously shot through her. Clamped between Bella's hand were Thor's fingers, turning pale from blood loss. Thor gritted his teeth and said nothing.

"I feel an urge to bear down," Bella whispered between quick puffs of breath.

"Ash, would you please call the doctor?" Dorie asked, and Ash quietly left the chamber. Dorie bathed Bella's face.

The doctor entered the room, cake crumbs dotting his waistcoat. "Well, my lady, have you finally decided to birth this babe? Everybody out while I examine her."

"*I* am not leaving," Thor declared.

"I wish Dorie to stay also," Bella hissed.

"My lady . . ."

"Go on with your examination, doctor," Thor instructed.

The doctor frowned, but pulled the bed covers back. "It is about time. We need the boiling water. The other items are ready."

"I shall ask the maid to bring the water up," Dorie said, and departed.

In the hall Ash slumped on a chair. He looked at Dorie, a question in his eyes. "The doctor says it is time. I must instruct the maid to bring the boiling water."

"I shall do that for you. When this is over, Dorie, we must talk."

She nodded and watched him descend the stairs. Sighing, she turned back to Bella's chamber.

As Bella's labor progressed, Dorie continued to

bathe her face in cold water while Thor held her hand. "Ah, I see the crown," the doctor recounted.

A green tint suffused Thor's pale face and his breath came fast and short. The doctor scowled at him. "Sit down, my lord. I do not need another patient."

"I am fine," Thor mumbled a second before he collapsed to the floor.

"Men!" Bella muttered, her voice filled with disgust. "Tell Ash to drag Thor out of my sight."

Dorie opened the door and said, "Ash, will you please come here?"

Ash jumped up from the chair where he slouched. "Me? You want me?"

"Yes. Bella wants something removed from the room that troubles her."

Ash strode in and stopped short. He stared at Thor. "Bloody hell!"

"Drag my swooning husband away, please," Bella declared.

Ash laughed. "I shall never let him forget this." Grasping his booted feet, Ash dragged him into the hall.

Suddenly a lusty cry filled the chamber. Dorie turned back to find the doctor holding the newborn by the feet. Once the doctor tied the umbilical cord, she quickly retrieved a blanket and swaddled the boy. "You have a son, my lady," the doctor informed Bella. "Wash him," the doctor instructed Dorie.

"Count his toes and fingers," Bella blurted.

Picking up each tiny hand with one finger, Dorie counted his fingers. "Ten perfect fingers."

Dorie silently counted again. "Ten perfect toes."

Dorie marveled at the exquisite tiny human being

chewing on his fist. Dorie brushed his pink cheek and tears welled in her eyes. How would it feel to hold Ash's babe in her arms? Wonderful!

Once she had him washed and in a clean blanket, Dorie laid the infant in Bella's arms. The doctor had already departed. Dorie cleaned Bella and put a clean nightdress on her as well as clean linen on the bed.

Once Bella was settled with her new son, Dorie said, "I shall get Thor."

Bella did not remove her eyes from her child. "Yes. Tell him to hurry to me."

Dorie rushed out of the room and almost tripped over Thor's body lying in the middle of the hall. "You left him in the hall?" she charged.

"Yes." He pointed to a pitcher on the table. "I was contemplating about whether to wake him."

Dorie smiled. "Wake him. Bella wishes her husband to join her."

Ash grinned. Picking up the pitcher, he dashed the water into Thor's face. Thor sputtered and shook his head. "What in the devil?" he yelled.

"Bella wishes you to join her and your child."

Thor sat up. "Is Bella well?" he demanded.

"She is quite well." Dorie smiled.

"And do I have a son or a daughter?"

"I think that is for her to tell you."

Thor vaulted up and surged into the chamber.

"I think he will be happy with his son," Dorie said.

Ash smiled. "Quite so. Now, madam, we have a few things to discuss."

"I must go see Hannah and Rose."

"After our discussion. You have a question to answer." Grabbing her wrist, Ash pulled her into a bedchamber.

"My lord!" she cried. The remaining words were lost as Ash claimed her lips in a kiss.

For a moment, Dorie stood stiffly, determined the kiss would not affect her. But as his lips caressed hers, her determination was forgotten and she sagged against him.

Ash raised his head. "I never did get my dance," he whispered, and began to twirl her around the room.

She clung to him, soft and warm. He stilled and kissed her again. "Ash, we cannot marry," Dorie whispered against his lips.

His thumb stroked her cheek. "Why not?"

"You are a marquess. You must marry someone of your own social standing."

"Social standing be damned. I do not want to marry some silly miss just out of the schoolroom. I want you," he murmured, and reclaimed her lips in a fierce kiss. Large hands squeezed her waist and pulled her closer. His burgeoning desire was evident. Dorie shuddered with yearning.

Was she a fool to deny him? She would never love again like she loved Ash. An angelic voice seemed to whisper in her ear, "Marry him. The man loves you."

The harder she attempted to fight the truth, the more it persisted. She loved Ash. He was her one, true love. There would never be another for her.

Dorie pulled away and gazed into the black flames of his eyes. "I love you, Ash."

He attempted to pull her back into his embrace, but she stopped him and paced to the fireplace. Unable to look at him, she stared into the banked embers and said, "That is not enough."

"Not enough?" he asked in bewilderment.

"I am afraid I am a very selfish person. I could never share you with other women." Now, he would walk away in disgust. He would never agree to a life of being tied to one woman.

Large hands settled on her shoulders and Ash kissed her neck. "Then you have nothing to fear, my love. One woman will do me a lifetime if she is you."

Dorie gasped and twirled to face him. "Are you certain?"

"Quite." He gently squeezed her shoulders. "Now I have vowed my love and my faithfulness. Will you marry me?"

Joy bubbled up in Dorie and a warm glow flowed through her. Maybe Christmas wishes really did come true. "Yes."

Ash exhaled a long sigh of contentment and kissed her hand. "You have made me the happiest man alive. There is only one thing I require."

Dorie cocked her head in question.

Ash grinned. "A special license. There will be no long engagement for you, my dear."

Dorie threw her arms around Ash and snuggled her face into his neck. "The shorter the better."

Ash's deep laughter filled the room. "I assume you informed Rose and Hannah of your earlier refusal."

Dorie nodded.

"Then shall we go share the news with them?"

"Yes," she whispered. Stepping away, Dorie placed her hand in his. "Lead on, my lord."

A GIFT OF LOVE

* * *

Lady Marwood looked up from her needlework. "I have not seen Hannah in hours. I assume she is in bed."

"No, I looked there first," Dorie informed her, and looked to where Vanora sat with a book open on her lap.

"I have not seen her in ages either."

Barrett entered the room. "I have the servants searching the entire house, Miss Knighton." His gaze shifted to Ash. "I checked your bedchamber myself, my lord. She was not there, nor was her doll in evidence."

"Doll?" Dorie asked.

Ash explained, "I gave her a doll as a birthday present." Turning back to the butler, he said, "Thank you, Barrett. Let me know if anything turns up."

Barrett bowed and departed.

Rose sat on the settee twisting her hands. "Where could she be?"

"It shows the child's lack of upbringing to cause such an inconvenience," Lady Marwood said. "When found, she should be whipped within an inch of her life. Thomas has behaved very rude also. He has disappeared."

Ash gritted his teeth. "Do not concern yourself, Lady Marwood."

Standing in the door, Barrett cleared his throat. "Beg your pardon, my lord. The magistrate is here asking for Lord Thorley and yourself."

"Show him in."

Fitzsimmons entered, his hat clutched between

beefy hands. "Sorry to disturb you, my lord. I'm sorry to say there has been an accident involving your cousin."

"Thomas?" Ash questioned. "I assumed he was abed."

Lady Marwood looked up. "He disappeared hours ago."

For the first time, Fitzsimmons noticed the other occupants in the chamber. "Will you excuse us, ladies? I need to speak with Lord Ashborne alone."

"Well!" Lady Marwood huffed, and lumbered to her feet. "Far be it from me to stay where I'm not wanted."

Ash looked at Dorie. "I would like for you and Rose to stay." Looking at Fitzsimmons, he explained, "Miss Knighton and I are betrothed."

Fitzsimmons's eyes opened wide in surprise. "My felicitations, my lord, Miss Knighton." After the door had closed, Fitzsimmons said, "He was making his way too fast in the dark and his carriage careened over a cliff. I'm afraid he is dead."

Ash collapsed onto the brocade settee. "Dead! Are you certain it is Thomas?"

Fitzsimmons nodded. "I've met Mr. Langford before."

"Hannah!" Dorie cried. "W-was there anyone with Thomas?"

"No, miss. He was driving the carriage himself. There was something odd, though." Fitzsimmons pulled a handkerchief-wrapped parcel out of his coat pocket.

"Mr. Langford had this on him. Does it belong to you, my lord?"

Ash took the parcel and untied the linen. He

A GIFT OF LOVE

stared at the items, his mouth agape. He gently touched each one. Diamond stickpin. Gold pocket watch. Silver filigree card holder.

"The cards have your name while the watch and handkerchief have your initials," Fitzsimmons explained.

"Yes, these are mine. But why would Thomas have them in his possession?"

"Where was the last place these articles were, to your knowledge?"

"In my bedchamber."

"Mayhap Thomas was the thief," Dorie suggested gently. "Barrett, have one of the servants check Thomas's bedchamber."

"Yes, miss."

Ash shook his head in disbelief and stared at Barrett's retreating back. "That is difficult to accept. Why would he do such an abhorrent deed?"

Dorie sat beside Ash and clasped his hand in hers. "Perhaps he had problems no one knew of."

Barrett entered the room. "All of Mr. Langford's clothing and toiletries are gone, my lord. I did find a note addressed to you." He handed Ash the folded, ivory vellum.

Ash's eyes perused the message. "Good Lord!"

Ash handed the vellum to Dorie. She gasped as her eyes followed the black writing.

Ash,
 I only have hours left since Hannah knows the truth. I have decided to journey to the Colonies where I will be safe from the reach of English law. I never wished to harm you or steal from Lord Thorley, but the money lenders threatened they would kill me if I

did not pay up. You are now betrothed and once you produce an heir, I shall never inherit your title or wealth.

Loosening the linchpins and ambushing you on your journey here were the acts of a desperate man. I pray you will forgive me for attempting your murder—twice now. And please ask Lord and Lady Thorley to forgive my thefts from their home.
Your cousin, Thomas

Dorie handed the vellum to Mr. Fitzsimmons. "Unbelievable!" she muttered.

Fitzsimmons clucked his tongue as he read the missive. "Mrs. Dorrington, I apologize for accusing you of the thefts. Apparently, my sources were very wrong and misguided."

Rose smiled shyly. "Apology accepted, sir."

"Mr. Fitzsimmons, since Thomas is dead, I hope we can keep these facts secret."

"Of course, my lord. No reason to sully a dead man's name, even if he is a blackguard. You can depend on me."

"Thank you. Have the local undertaker coffin him. I will take him home to the family vault."

Fitzsimmons nodded. "I'm right sorry about all this, my lord." He turned toward the door and let himself out.

Ash shook his head. "I cannot believe it!"

Barrett cleared his throat from the doorway. "Miss Knighton, we have discovered your sister."

Standing beside Barrett was Hannah, her dress torn and cobwebs in her hair. She clutched a doll to her chest.

Dorie bounded up and pulled Hannah into her

arms. "I have been worried sick about you." Grasping her by the shoulders, Dorie demanded, "Where have you been?"

"Hiding in the attic. I'm sorry you were worried."

"But why were you hiding in the attic?"

"I went into Ash's room to retrieve my doll and Mr. Langford was there." Hannah chewed on her bottom lip. "He was stealing Ash's belongings. H-he chased me. You, Ash, and Lord and Lady Thorley were busy. I didn't trust anyone else. So I hid from him. Did Lady Thorley have her baby?"

Dorie smiled and brushed a cobweb from Hannah's cheek. "Yes. A son. It is time for you to go to bed, young lady."

"I shall see to her," Rose replied, and led her upstairs.

Dorie tugged on Ash's hand. "You shall feel better after a good night's sleep yourself."

"I suppose," Ash uttered, and stood. Smiling slightly, he added, "Will you be offended if I ask you to stay with me tonight? I do not relish being alone."

Heat infused Dorie's cheeks and she wrapped her arms around Ash's neck. "Not at all, my lord. I do not relish being away from you. I look forward to spending every night with you."

Ash grinned. His hands squeezed her waist and pulled her closer. "Tomorrow I shall obtain a special license. The local vicar can marry us posthaste." Gently, his lips brushed hers.

A thought skittered through Dorie's mind. She must thank Hannah's angel for answering her wishes. She had indeed obtained a loving husband.

Epilogue

Seven days later

Hannah peered over the edge of the bassinet to spy the new son of Lord Thorley. With one finger, she brushed one tiny hand, and it closed around her finger.

"You're special," she whispered. "You were born on Christmas Day and you have your own special angel. When you get older, I shall instruct you on the aspects of your Christmas angel."

Solemn eyes stared at her and she smiled. "My angel even found Dorie a husband. Ash is to be your godfather also."

The responsibility weighed heavily on her shoulders. She must make sure he understood.

"Hannah," Dorie whispered from the door, "what are you doing?"

"Saying good-bye. He was born on Christmas Day just like me."

"Yes. Are you ready to travel to our new home in Dorset?"

Hannah nodded and looked at Dorie. "It is a

shame we have to leave our nice little cottage. Is Ash's home nice?"

"From his description, yes, it is very nice. It is *our* home now, but we shall come back to visit."

"Does Ash mind very much getting me and Aunt Rose in the bargain?" Hannah whispered.

Dorie smiled and smoothed Hannah's hair. "Not at all. He loves you both very much."

Hannah returned her smile. "I am glad. It will all be so very exciting. I've never seen the ocean."

"Yes, there are many new experiences awaiting us in Dorset."

"What in the devil is taking you so long?" Ash asked from the doorway. "I would like to arrive in Dorset before the new year is finished."

Hannah skipped to him and hugged him. "I am ready," she announced, and skipped down the hall.

Dorie paused, looking down at the child. Strong hands settled on her shoulders. "And what are you thinking, my love?"

"How thrilled I shall be when we have a child."

Ash kissed the nape of her neck. "Me too."

Dorie laughed. "Just promise me you will not swoon."

"I promise, but you must promise to be nice to me when the time comes."

Dorie turned and her arms encircled Ash's waist. Pillowing her head on his shoulder, she said, "I shall strive my best to be sweet-tempered during childbirth. I'm the luckiest woman in the world. But tell me the truth. Did *you* leave the gifts on the doorstep?"

"Does it really matter, my love? I'm the luckiest man."

But Dorie knew it was not luck she had to thank. A miracle had taken place and brought her love and a lifetime of happiness. And when she and Ash had children of their own, every Christmas she would tell them the story of the Christmas miracle and the gift of love.

About the Author

Deborah has been an avid reader from a very young age. As a teenager she spent more time with books than with boys. Gothics, Grace Livingston Hill, and romances were her companions.

Deborah lives in central Alabama with her husband David, where she has a day job with the government and looks forward to writing full-time one day soon. She has a fondness for chocolate, cats, and reading, of course!

There is something magical about sharing charactrers from your own imagination. Deborah hopes you enjoy this story and wishes you romance in your own life.

Visit Deborah's web page at:
http://www.heartofdixie.org/pages/matthews.html